WESLEY: AN EYE FOR AN EYE

GEORGE D. DURRANT AND SUSAN EASTON BLACK

IMMORTAL WORKS
SALT LAKE CITY

Immortal Works LLC
1505 Glenrose Drive
Salt Lake City, Utah 84104
Tel: (385) 202-0116

Cover Art by Ashley Literski
http://strangedevotion.wixsite.com/strangedesigns

This book is a work of fiction. Names, characters, businesses, organizations, places, events and incidents either are the product of the author's imagination or are used fictitiously. Any resemblance to actual persons, living or dead, events, or locales is entirely coincidental.

ISBN 978-1-953491-52-7 (Paperback)
ASIN B0BXJ5ZRX3 (Kindle)

To our pickleball friends
and the Wesley in each of us

INTRODUCTION

Small towns that dominated the American landscape in the 1920s are gone. Urban sprawl has replaced the link to farm and family and a sense of belonging. Apartment dwellings, transit systems, and electronic devices have become the norm instead of visits to Grandma's house, the horse and buggy, and neighborly chats across the fence. Gossip, infighting, and inbreeding that defined America's small towns have been supplanted by snippets of national news in the name of progress.

As expected, the stories that defined small towns have been crushed under the weight of expansionism. But there is one story from the 1920's that has refused to succumb to big-city life. It is a story of mystery, romance, and insanity. The setting is Rooster Creek, Utah, and the star is an unlikely, small man named Wesley Birch, who scared even the bravest of men in town. It wasn't his fanatic religious zeal that was frightening; it was his irrational behavior.

No matter how the story of Wesley is told, no listener exits the room, for none wants to miss the twists and turns of the tale. The story of Wesley always begins the same way: in a hotel lobby.

1

THE HOTEL LOBBY

Wesley turned the knob and entered the lobby of the Rigby Hotel, a room half the size of a boxcar. An electric lightbulb dangled from the ceiling, a tattered rag rug covered the middle of the wood-planked floor, and a couch, overlaid with a patchwork quilt, hugged the back wall. The night clerk sat on the only chair in the room behind a makeshift desk. He was in a heated discussion with a middle-aged, barrel-shaped man dressed in an orange checkered suit.

Wesley looked out the door and shouted, "Hurry up, Lydia. We're home."

"Welcome to the Rigby Hotel," the clerk said, forcing a smile and pretending to be glad that a strange old man and his daughter had come to the hotel at such a late hour.

"Got any rooms left?" Wesley asked. "We need one with two beds."

"Sure do," the clerk replied without looking up from the registry lying open in front of him. "Be with you in a minute."

To the man in the checkered suit, the clerk said, "This is the last time I'll ask. Sir, I need your name."

"My name is none of your business. I'll pay cash."

The clerk stiffened, sat up straight, and glared at him. "Sir," he said, "with all due respect, give me your name or get out."

"John Doe."

The clerk shook his head and sighed. "That'll be a buck."

The orange-clad man offered a silver coin.

The clerk took the coin and put it in a cigar box before handing the man a key. "Can I help you with those bags?"

"Don't touch anything! I've got expensive photography equipment. I don't want a clumsy hotel clerk breaking something."

"You a photographer?" Wesley asked.

"No, I'm a plumber. Just carry this stuff for exercise. Of course, I'm a photographer! Geez, does anybody in this hick town have a brain? Been here all day trying to take photos in the back of the drugstore. Had two customers. Spent the last six hours in the pool hall schooling the locals on the game and taking their money. In the morning, I'm moving on to California. In Hollywood, folks aren't as stingy as they are in this nowhere dump Chicken Hollow, or whatever you call the town."

The night clerk had spent all of his twenty years in Rooster Creek. He knew the town was far from perfect, but he was not about to let a man in an orange checkered suit insult his town. He could overlook a guest belittling Lehi or Pleasant Grove, as such criticism was warranted, but not his Rooster Creek. The clerk tightened his fist and clenched his teeth, causing his prominent chin to protrude. Sensing danger, the photographer moved back a half step.

"He who taketh up the sword shall perish by the sword," Wesley said. Strangely, Wesley's words calmed the situation as the clerk and guest stared at him. The clerk slumped back in his chair, his fist relaxing. He still wanted to hit the man but reasoned it wasn't worth losing his job.

Believing he'd prevented the first blow in the Battle of Armageddon, Wesley sat down triumphant on the worn couch. Lydia, a bit unnerved by what she'd seen, sat next to him. Her eyes followed the photographer as he moved to the stairs.

Sensing her gaze, the photographer looked back. "Who are you? I've taken pictures of gorgeous women, but I've never seen the likes of you. Your face puts Hollywood dames to shame."

Lydia turned her head to the side. Seemingly unaware that other guests were sleeping upstairs, the man called to her in a voice dark with innuendos. "And, sweetheart, if you need somewhere to stay, there's a place in my room. Be quick about it. I've got an early train to catch." The photographer punctuated his offensive invitation by letting his hungry eyes rake over Lydia.

Wesley jumped up and called upon the powers of heaven to send fire and brimstone to smite the lecherous photographer. The night clerk leaped from behind the desk with fists clenched.

"Hey, mister," the clerk growled. "We don't talk to ladies like that in this hotel."

"Who says?" The photographer sneered.

"I say. If you want to stay here, act like a gentleman."

The photographer stared at the clerk, who now looked more like a giant than a man. He lowered his head, picked up his bags, and climbed the rickety staircase. Satisfied there would be no more trouble, the clerk retook his seat behind the desk.

Three steps up the stairs and safely out of the clerk's gasp, the photographer shouted, "I'm in 202, beautiful. When that ugly clerk falls asleep, come on over."

The clerk lifted both hands in the air in disbelief. "I'm sorry about this," he said to Wesley and Lydia. "Some people... You know? Now, sir, what can I do for you and your daughter?"

Wesley slowly walked from the couch to the desk. He exhaled deeply as if he'd encountered the assumption of his being Lydia's father a hundred times. "She's my sister."

"Oh, I see," the clerk replied. "I apologize. With that long beard, I took you for an older man."

"That's all right. Thanks for what you said to that excuse of a Christian. What we need in this world are more men like you who stand up to evil villains like that orange Philistine."

"Just thought he should show a little respect for the lady. I apologize for losing my temper." Dipping his pen in the inkwell, the clerk asked, "Name?"

"Wesley Birch."

"The lady's name?"

"Lydia Birch."

"Spell that, please."

"L-y-d-i-a."

The clerk wrote her name in the hotel registry. "Now, let's see. What else do we need? Oh yeah, the date." He spoke aloud as he wrote. "September 6, 1922." Lifting his head, the clerk said, "I'll put you two in room 208, the best room in the hotel tonight. It's a long hallway away from the photographer's room." He handed Wesley the key.

"You know our names. What's yours?" Wesley asked.

The young clerk smiled sheepishly. "I should have told you. My name is Jed Dawson." He extended his hand.

Lydia watched the clerk shake Wesley's hand but said nothing. She could not take her eyes off him. He wasn't just tall, he was ruggedly handsome. Jed, in turn, got his first good look at Lydia, now lit by the fullness of the dangling lightbulb. He gulped audibly, opened his eyes wide, and asked, "And you're Lydia?" As the two clasped hands, Lydia felt the roughness of his weather-worn skin and the firm pressure of his grip. Jed held her hand a second longer than courtesy required. As he pulled his hand, he turned away, but just as quickly, he looked back.

"I'll carry your suitcases up those old stairs," Jed said. "We're going to build new steps next month."

"No," Wesley replied. "We can manage just fine."

"Are you sure?"

"Yes. Are you the owner of the Rigby Hotel?"

"I'm working at night to earn extra money. Getting married soon."

Wesley ignored Jed's comment about marriage. "What do you do during the day?"

"I'm a farmer. I grew up on a chicken farm a few blocks from here and have been working on the farm ever since."

Wesley leaned forward. "A farmer?" he asked. "You own the farm?"

"My father owns a small farm, or, rather, the bank owns it, but someday, if my father doesn't lose it, the farm will be mine."

Jed moved forward and again offered to carry the bags.

Motioning for Jed to stand back, Wesley said, "We can manage. I have the strength of ten because my heart is pure. Sampson has little over me."

As Wesley and Lydia climbed the stairs, Jed called out to them. "Screw the light bulb in, and it will light up your room. There's a toilet at the end of the hall and a sink."

Lydia pulled her dress up a little above her boot tops to better climb the narrow stairs. When she looked back, she was pleased Jed was watching. She ascended the stairs and walked out of sight.

As she disappeared into the darkness, Jed's shock at seeing such a beauty left him frozen in place. His eyes blinked faster than the frames of a movie, and his heart beat like the sound of galloping hooves pounding turf. With his right hand, he stroked his curly black hair as if trying to press it down into his skull. With his trembling left hand, he pulled a red handkerchief from his pocket and wiped his nose.

"I can't believe my eyes," he whispered. "The most beautiful woman in the world standing here in the lobby. I talked to her. I shook hands with her. She would be the perfect match for Karl."

A quieter thought crept in—*Could she be the perfect match for me? The thought was quickly crowded out. Me? The son of the town drunk and a cleaning lady—not likely. I spend most of my time gathering eggs and cleaning out chicken coops. Ugliest guy in town, a real farm hick. No chance for me.* Yet ever the optimist, Jed grinned as he whispered, "Then again, seems like she held my hand just a moment or maybe two longer than needed. But...I'm marrying Matilda on Saturday."

Matilda's eyes had filled with love and trust the day he proposed marriage. Her eyes had warmed him then, but now thinking of Matilda was like pouring cold water on his heart. *What if Matilda looked like Lydia?* he asked himself. Matilda wasn't a beauty. She was pretty in her own way, but she wasn't the sort of woman who turns a man's head. With a heavy sigh, Jed walked to the couch, rested his hands behind his head, and fantasized of what might have been.

2

GO TO HIM, LITTLE SISTER

In the privacy of room 208, Lydia got ready for bed. She uncoiled her hair and watched the tendrils cascade into a half circle on the worn, laundered blanket. She lay down on the bed and pulled a heavy blanket over her head to create a private space for her thoughts.

As Wesley lay in the other bed, his mind swirled with hope, causing the thin-lipped corners of his mouth to stretch into a broad grin. "The Lord has provided a farmer," he said aloud. Like a distant drum getting closer and closer, he chanted, "A farmer. A farmer." Before he finished, he envisioned the wedding of Lydia and Jed—such a beautiful couple.

Unable to sleep with Wesley's chants and visions of marital bliss, Lydia's private muses ran the gauntlet from hope to despair. Lydia pushed back the blanket, stood, and walked across the room to check the door latch. Fears of Frank Cromwell were never far from her mind. She glanced under the bed as if he were hiding there but then quickly pulled the blanket over her head again, turned on her side, and closed her eyes.

Minutes later and half-asleep, she heard Wesley whisper, "Lydia."

She didn't respond, but when he called her name again, she protested. "Go to sleep."

Wesley was wide awake. He had a revelation that must be told. He threw off his blanket and stood right above Lydia, who had purposely faced away from him, and thundered, "That man, Jed Dawson, is the farmer, Lydia. He's the man the Lord has prepared for you. No time to sleep now. I could tell right away that young feller likes the looks of you. Did you see him stare at you? What do you think of him?"

"I think you're a fool. Go back to bed. In the morning, the night clerk will be gone, and so will we. We will never see him again. Besides, didn't you hear him say he's getting married?"

"But, Lydia, we have *all night*. He's the night clerk. He has to stay awake *all night*. Go downstairs and keep him company. You have time on your side. With time and the Lord, everything will work out as planned."

Lydia hated the high pitch of Wesley's voice when he got excited. "Quit talking like that, Wesley. I'm not going downstairs. Do you hear me? I'm not going downstairs."

"Come on, Lydia," Wesley pleaded. "The Lord has provided this man for you just like He provided Adam for Eve. Go downstairs and claim him. Have faith, sister. Have faith. The Lord moves in mysterious ways, His wonders to perform. I'll be praying all the time you are with him."

Though it was more of an attempt to get away from Wesley than a sign she was listening, Lydia stood and, with hands on her hips, glared at her brother. "You go down to the lobby if you've got so much faith," she said. "Tell Jed Dawson to marry me, in the name of the Lord."

"That's ridiculous, and you know it," Wesley said. "Why can't you act rationally for once? If you don't go downstairs tonight, you will be with me for the next twenty years. Is that what you want, Lydia? Is it? Is it?"

"No! That's not what I want."

"Tell him I snore so loud you can't sleep. Ask him if you can sleep on the couch in the lobby. Take a pillow and a blanket with you. Now go to him, little sister, and be blessed."

Lydia lay back on her bed. "I'm so tired," she whispered. "My whole body aches from sitting on the train for so many hours. I want to sleep, Wesley. Let me have my peace."

"Jesus was up all night before he walked on the Sea of Galilee. You must go downstairs."

As emotions from the last several days boiled to the surface, Lydia cringed and began to cry.

Wesley put his hand on her shoulder. "Don't cry. You always cry. Crying doesn't solve anything. You must do this. In the name of the Lord, I command you to gird up your loins and go to the lobby. The Lord can't bless an unwilling servant. Stand and walk."

Wesley reached for Lydia's arm and pulled her out of bed. Lydia felt the familiar clawing hopelessness that had haunted her since their parents' deaths. Knowing she had no choice but to obey her tyrannical brother, she resentfully said, "It will take me a few minutes to put my hair up."

"He's going to be your husband. It's all right if he sees your hair down. It's your crowning glory."

As Lydia braided her hair, she asked herself, *When did I lose my will to this tyrant? Why do I obey his every command?* Impatiently, Wesley paced back and forth, hovering over Lydia and making demands. "Make it quick. A ram can only be kept so long in the thicket."

With her hair pinned in an elaborate coil at the base of her neck, Lydia moved toward the door. Wesley smiled triumphantly and put his hands on her shoulders. "Come now, sister. Put a smile on your face. A farmer doesn't want to marry a solemn woman."

With that, he picked up the pillow and blanket from the bed and placed them in her arms. He opened the door, put his hand on her back, and pressed her out into the dark hallway.

Lydia hadn't moved an inch before Wesley closed the door behind her, rubbed his hands together, and said, "Dear Lord, may thy spirit be with Lydia and the night clerk." Feeling the night chill, he hurried to his bed, pulled the blanket snuggly over his head, and fell fast asleep.

Jed was lying on the couch, skimming through a Montgomery Ward catalog, when he heard an upstairs door open and close. As he listened, he thought to himself that someone was likely heading to the bathroom at the end of the upstairs hall. When the footsteps stopped, Jed raised his head slightly off the couch and listened more closely. He sensed the presence of someone at the top of the stairs. He sat up, watching intently as a person appeared in the darkness. To his astonishment, it was the beautiful woman he checked into the hotel less than an hour before. He sat motionless, silently watching.

Out of the dark stillness, she spoke. "I woke up. Please, forgive me."

Jed did not reply as Lydia walked slowly down the last few stairs. Just an hour or so ago, her appearance had aroused excitement and fantasy. Seeing her now in a nightgown brought a shiver of fear and a faint whiff of guilt. "Something wrong?" he asked stiffly as he shoved the catalog under the couch cushion.

Wesley's lie slipped easily from Lydia's lips. "I can't sleep. My brother snores. I'll just...sleep on the rug." She moved toward the tattered rug covering the floor planks.

"I don't think that would be... Could you wake him up? It would be better if you stayed upstairs," Jed mumbled, feeling uncomfortable and perplexed at this unusual turn of events.

"I understand. I didn't want to..." Lydia's words trailed off as she took three deep breaths and turned back to the stairs.

Jed sensed Lydia's distress went beyond a snoring brother. "I wish you could stay down here, but it's—it's against the rules." *Does the hotel really have rules about where a guest sleeps?* He didn't know.

But it doesn't seem right to have a woman with me all alone. Then again, it doesn't seem right to turn her away.

"I'll move to the chair behind the desk," Jed continued. "You can sleep on the couch. And if we don't talk—if nobody knows—I'm sure it will be fine."

Lydia had already begun to ascend the stairs, but she looked over her right shoulder at Jed. "Will you get in trouble because of—" Her voice choked on the last word. "Me?"

Jed stood, the sound of tears jolting him into being the considerate gentleman he always tried to be around the fairer sex. "No, no, no! I think it will be all right."

Now it was Lydia who hesitated. "It will not be all right. I should never have come down here. My brother, he gets these crazy ideas. He feels responsible for me. He's my guardian, so I have no choice but to do what he says. If he says to come down here, I come down."

"He told you to come down to the lobby? Why?"

Lydia didn't meet Jed's curious gaze. "Wesley says the Lord speaks to him and tells him what to do. He said the Lord told him—I can't tell you what he said the Lord told him. I can't do this anymore. You're a good man. Forget this." Lydia swirled away, poised to disappear into the upstairs darkness.

"Forget what?"

Lydia bowed her head in silence. She wanted to tell him, but he might think she was as crazy as Wesley. Her body convulsed slightly as she raised her arm to wipe her eyes on the long sleeve of her nightgown. Across the room, Jed could tell she was crying. He wondered what was going on. Was this woman in trouble or in danger from her brother? Lydia slowly took a step higher on the stairs. Jed was about to let her go up the rickety staircase. That would have been the wise thing to do, and yet, like carefully speaking to a frightened child, he asked, "What did he say? Maybe I can help. Does he hurt you?"

"My brother says the Lord told him that you are the man I should marry. He told me to come down here and claim you."

Jed was dumbfounded. He sat on the couch.

"Wesley would not take no for an answer," Lydia continued. "If you knew Wesley, you would know he's obsessed with making sure I follow his prophecies. Sometimes it turns out good for me, but most of the time, it's terrible. If I go back to the room now, I can tell him that I tried. Jed, that's your name, right? Forget this. Pretend it never happened."

"Where are you going tomorrow?"

"Who knows," Lydia replied. Her words sounded cold and hollow.

"Look, I don't want to be like your brother, telling you what to do, but I do want you to come back down," Jed said. "The least I can do is give you a good night's sleep."

Lydia remained motionless for another moment before stepping off the stairs. Head bowed, she crossed the room to stand near Jed. For a brief second in the dimly lit room, she looked up, and the two young, confused people gazed into each other's eyes. This time it was not beauty that Jed saw, nor the prophesied farmer that Lydia saw. In that quiet moment, each caught a brief glimpse of the compassionate heart of the other. Jed, who so often felt and acted like a boy, was in that moment, a man—a good man.

"Here's the couch," he said as he moved to the chair behind the desk. "It's not much, but it's all yours. I promise I won't snore."

His attempt at a joke caused them both to laugh. For the first time in a long time, Lydia felt understood.

Several minutes passed, and all he heard in the lobby was the chirp of crickets outside. Jed liked the sound. It reminded him of childhood campouts with his best friend, Karl Ward. But not all his childhood memories were pleasant. His alcoholic father left him physically and emotionally scarred. Perhaps that was why his feelings were tender when he considered possible abuse. He thought Lydia should be filled with confidence and joy. But even at their first meeting, he sensed that was not the case. Instead, she seemed filled with pain and sorrow.

He recalled a dog following him home from school one day when he was a small boy. When he tried to chase the dog away, it cowered and lay on its back in a show of submission. Jed thought the dog's former owner must have beaten all the happiness out of the dog. He brought the dog home. It was one of the few times Jed went against the will of his father. He got a black eye and a split lip for his defiance, but in the end, his father let him keep the dog.

Lydia reminded him of that cowering dog as he watched her settle into the couch.

With time on his hands, Jed's mind whirled and spun. He thought of Matilda—wonderful Matilda, the best woman who'd ever set foot in Rooster Creek. He reckoned that he was the luckiest man in the world to soon claim her as his bride. Matilda was confident and able to meet life head-on. She had not been trampled by senseless cruelty. Love was all Matilda saw in her home, and love was all she gave. Lydia was different—so uncertain, so weak, so abused.

How would it be to be married to such a beautiful, kind, and tender woman? He regretted not meeting Lydia before committing to Matilda.

Across the room, Lydia was silent, but she was not sleeping. She, too, was caught up in thoughts that blocked her from slumber. *Could Wesley be right?* Lydia thought. *Could the Lord have brought this good man to me? Yet how could a man like Jed Dawson be interested in a woman who had nothing but loss and emptiness inside?* As fatigue overcame her, Lydia fell into the only place she could find peace—sleep.

3

YOUNG LOVE

Ahalf hour later, Lydia awoke, sure Frank Cromwell was standing near the couch. Her scream for help startled Jed, who was half-asleep. He saw Lydia shielding her head with her hands from an unseen assailant. He rushed to her side.

"Are you all right?"

Lydia, still dazed from sleep, grasped Jed's outstretched hands. "Frank Cromwell was here. Is he still here?"

"Who's Frank Cromwell?"

"I knew he would find me. Where can I hide?"

Jed tenderly squeezed her delicate hands in his. "You were dreaming. There is no one here. Just you and me. You're safe."

After searching Jed's eyes, Lydia let go of his hands. Trying to explain her behavior, she said, "Frank wanted to marry me. I refused. The dream seemed so real."

"You're safe here. If Frank ever comes to the Rigby Hotel, he'll wish he hadn't. Go back to sleep. You have nothing to fear."

Lydia sighed. "I can't sleep now. Could we talk about you?" She thought for a moment. "Have you always lived here?"

"Born and raised in Rooster Creek," Jed said. "Reckon I'll die here too. It's like the locals say, 'If you get on in Rooster Creek, you get off in Rooster Creek.'"

"Do you like it here?"

"It's home—all I've ever known. Good place to raise a family. Matilda wants a dozen kids."

Seeing that his words had a calming effect on Lydia, Jed walked back to his seat behind the desk and sat down. "Everybody likes Matilda," he continued. "I wish she was here. I honestly don't know what she sees in me."

"She's a lucky woman."

"She's no movie star," Jed said. "Not like you but a good woman." The words died on his lips, and he sat in silence with his head bowed. "Well, enough about me. What about you, Lydia? There must be other men besides Frank Cromwell in your life."

"Afraid not."

"Well, seeing as I'm already taken," Jed said with a wink, "You should meet my friend Karl Ward. Karl and I grew up arguing over who would marry the prettiest girl. If he married you, he'd win by a mile. He came in town today to be the best man at my wedding. If you and your brother stay a few more days, I'll introduce you. Karl's great-grandfather was one of the first settlers in Rooster Creek. When he and eleven other pioneers came to this place and bedded down for the night, they were awakened in the morning by the crowing of a single rooster. His great-grandpa called the place Rooster Creek. The name stuck, and so did Great-Grandpa Ward. He started a bank. Karl's grandfather inherited the bank. Then he gave the bank to Karl's father, who is the mayor and the richest man in town. Mr. Ward gave my dad a job cleaning his bank. When dad was too drunk to do the job, he didn't fire him; he kept on paying him. I guess you could say Karl's father is like a father to me."

"Why do you talk so much of Karl and his family?"

With that question, Lydia threw a spotlight on Jed's darkest insecurities. He had long considered himself second class to Karl and most others in town.

Knowing she had struck a nerve, Lydia looked away. She had no desire to hurt this gentle man. "I'm sorry, Jed. Who am I to ask such a question? And yet you..." She didn't finish.

Jed swallowed and placed his hand on his brow. He blew out a puff of air before saying, "Karl would be good for you. I wouldn't."

"I'll be the judge of that," Lydia said. Impulsively, she walked to the desk and put her hand on Jed's shoulder. "Don't get me wrong. I'm not suggesting there could ever be anything between us—you're engaged. I just wonder why you think Karl would be better for me than you."

"Look at me," Jed said. "I'm the biggest hick in Rooster Creek. Going no place. Big ugly guy—about as smart as a rock."

"Do you ever look in a mirror?" she asked. "You are a handsome man. You're really tall. You have broad shoulders and deep blue eyes. You are sensitive and kind. No more of this 'poor me' nonsense."

Jed pulled a worn hanky from his pocket and wiped his eyes. He could not believe that a beautiful woman like Lydia could see him as anything but a Utah hick. Hoping to change the subject, Jed asked, "What's your story? You are so beautiful, yet you seem sad."

Overcome with the memories of past burdens, Lydia covered her face with her hands and sobbed. "There's no hope for me."

Before Jed could offer a rebuttal, a horse whinnied.

"Is that your horse?" Lydia asked.

"He's out back."

"Can I see him?"

"Sure."

Jed stood up, opened the front door, and walked with Lydia around the side of the hotel to the water trough in the back.

When Lydia spotted Eliminator, she hurried past Jed. "Look at him. He's majestic."

"He's a palomino," Jed said. "Karl's father bought him for me when he was just a colt. I fell in love with him the first time I saw him. Next to Karl, Eliminator is my best friend."

Jed stroked the animal's nose. "You and I are friends, right, big fella?"

"Look at his eyes," Lydia said. "I think horses know everything about everything. They just don't want to talk about it. Isn't that right, Eliminator?" She leaned forward. "Can he run fast?"

"Fast enough to beat every horse in town."

"Could he win the Kentucky Derby?"

"Could you win the derby, old fella?" Jed asked, patting Eliminator on the back.

The horse raised his head and whinnied with confidence. "He thinks he could, but he's no Donerail."

Lydia didn't mean to say the words aloud, but she couldn't hold them back. "Jed, I think..."

Jed looked at Lydia and whispered, "You too."

Lydia smiled at him and took his hands in hers. They twirled around as if dancers but just as suddenly let go. They walked back to the hotel lobby without saying a word.

It was Jed who broke the silence. "You may want to get some rest before the rooster crows."

"Rooster?"

"We've had an official town rooster ever since we've had a town. Each new official rooster is a direct descendant of the first. He's our official waker-upper."

"One rooster wakes up the whole town?"

"Rooster Creek is a little town."

Lydia laughed.

When the rooster finally did crow, Jed and Lydia knew their night together had come to an end. Jed reached out his hand, and Lydia extended hers.

"I'll never forget you," Jed said. "And if, uh...if you'll let me, I'll love you forever."

Jed opened his arms wide so that Lydia could wrap her arms around his waist and melt against him. They held each other for a long time. Jed looked down at her beautiful face, his eyes asking a silent question he could never voice. Seeing the answer he hoped for, he bent his head, and their lips met. A moment later, they reluctantly backed away. Standing apart was not what either of them wanted.

The rooster crowed again. The small room began to glow in the early morning sunshine.

Jed turned away from Lydia and moved to the chair, where he lowered his head until it rested on his forearm. Lydia sat down on the couch. They were as still as statues. Jed recalled being thrown to the ground by a horse. The physical pain of that long-ago day was easier to bear than the choking pain he felt now.

Seeing the agony on his face, Lydia said, "In twenty years, you'll know that by our backing away from each other, you opened the door to a glorious future with Matilda and those twelve children."

"What about your future?" Jed asked.

Lydia fidgeted with the corner of her sleeve, not meeting his eyes. "I've had many chances to practice getting over things. I've turned it into quite an art."

As Lydia looked up and met his gaze, Jed saw in her shuttered eyes that she'd begun to forget him already, laying a wall between them, brick by brick.

"I'll go upstairs, wake up Wesley, and tell him his prophecy missed the mark. He'll blame me and act like a madman. After a tirade of curses and threats of fire and brimstone, he'll receive a revelation that we need to leave Rooster Creek and keep heading to California. In an hour we'll be gone—heading west."

Lydia moved toward the stairs, leaving Jed to wistfully watch her walk away, unable to ask her to stay.

4

THE WEDDING PHOTOGRAPH

"Did that foulmouthed rooster wake you folks up too?" the photographer yelled from the top of the stairs. "Good grief. Five o'clock is an obscene hour to be awakened, out of bed, and carrying oversized bags down these narrow stairs. Somebody should cook that buzzard for Sunday dinner."

Stepping into the lobby, the orange-clad photographer gasped as he looked at Lydia in her nightgown. "Been up all night with the night clerk have you, missy? You can do better than that ugly giant. I best go upstairs and tell your old man."

"No!" Lydia said.

Rubbing the scruffy hairs on his chin as only an uncouth man could, the photographer said, "I can keep your secret if you let me take a photograph of you. A photo of a ravening beauty would help my business. I could tell every ugly old hag that you once looked like them, but with my extraordinary darkroom techniques, they could look just like you, darling—the prettiest woman I've ever seen."

Before the photographer could change his mind and spill their secret to Wesley, Lydia said, "I'll go upstairs and put on a dress."

"A nightgown works for me," the photographer said.

Lydia ran past Jed up the stairs and tiptoed down the hall in hopes of not waking Wesley. Inside room 208, she quietly rummaged through her carpetbag to find her pink Sunday dress. With garment in hand, she hurried out of the room to the bathroom, where she took a minute to put on her outfit and freshen up.

When Lydia walked down the stairs dressed in her finest, the photographer, who had spent the last few moments berating the hotel and its night clerk with shameless intensity, stood speechless.

"You're gorgeous," Jed said.

"You'll love me forever, right?" Lydia asked.

"Don't tell me you're marrying him," the photographer said, pointing a finger at Jed.

"Of course not!" Lydia said. "Where should I stand for the photograph?"

"By the window. Light from the window will give you an angelic look."

As Lydia stood near the window, gazing at the morning rays, the photographer adjusted and readjusted his camera. With a flash, he took the photo. Feeling pleased with himself, he motioned to Jed. "Bring that chair next to the beauty, sit down, take off that stupid hotel badge, and then square your shoulders. You're going to be in a photo with a real pretty woman—I'll make this a beauty-and-the-beast photograph. Act proud about it. And you, gorgeous, smooth the folds of your dress. Put your right hand on lover boy's shoulder. Yes, just like that. Now, hold still. This has the makings of a portrait of a beautiful bride and groom if it weren't for you, cowboy. I can see the sign now: *Get your wedding photos here.* Blushing bride and lucky hick."

With another flash of light and without another word, the photographer returned to room 202 to develop the film. Although it was an elaborate process, he was quick about it. When he entered the lobby again, the photographer held two photographs in his hand. The first was of Lydia standing in the early morning light near the window. The second he disgustedly handed to Jed. "I can't use this.

Didn't you hear me say to take off the hotel badge? No one will believe this is a wedding photo." In a voice laced with sarcasm, he said, "Good luck on your marriage." Turning to Lydia, he said, "Good luck explaining to your old man why you were in the lobby with the clerk all night. You'll excuse me for stealing a kiss from the blushing bride before I leave."

"No chance of that," Jed said. "Get out!"

When the photographer was nearly at the door, a loud voice boomed from the top of the stairs. "Marriage? Is it you, Lydia? You and the farmer?"

"Yes!" the photographer shouted. "Show him the wedding photo of the happy bride and groom."

With that, the man was out the door. Wesley rushed down the stairs, snatching the photograph out of Jed's hand. As Wesley gazed at the photo, he said, "You have my permission to marry Lydia. You have my approval. You are the ram in the thicket who has been claimed."

Jed pulled himself away from Wesley's bony grasp and grabbed the photograph out of his hand. As Wesley turned to express his wondrous joy to Lydia, Jed placed the photograph carefully in the desk drawer under the registry. As he looked back at Lydia, he saw her place her hands firmly on Wesley's shoulders.

"Jed Dawson is going to marry Matilda. He loves Matilda. They are going to have twelve children. Ask the Lord to help you find another farmer for me. And calm down so you don't wake the hotel guests."

Instead of heeding her words, Wesley bolted out the lobby door to Main Street. He ran back and forth in front of the hotel, shouting. "Wake up! I have news! My sister is marrying a farmer. Like Eve found Adam, Lydia found Jed."

Lydia ran outside to stop Wesley. "Get back inside! You're acting crazy. I'm not getting married."

Jed's face drained of all color as he watched the siblings quarrel. His frame shook like leaves on an aspen tree as fear fueled his thoughts. *How can you reason with such a man? What if someone hears him? He'll tell the whole town. The gossip on the street will be, 'Did you hear big dumb Jed, the son of the town drunk, promised to marry some floozy who spent the night with him in the hotel?' Townsfolk will swarm around Wesley, eager to hear his tale. What will Matilda think? How will I ever explain this?*

The warmth Jed felt for Lydia chilled in his veins. "Lydia, stop him!" he cried out to her. "He's your brother; make him stop!"

"There's nothing I can do," Lydia shouted back. "Wesley will rant and rave for an hour or more. He will run from one end of Main Street to the other, telling everyone about the marriage. Our only hope is to take him someplace where no one can hear him."

"Geneva Resort. Nobody will be there this early. I'll get the hotel buggy!"

"Hurry! I'll stay with Wesley and try to calm him down."

Mrs. Rigby, although startled at being awakened at such an early hour, was accommodating and wanted to hear more about the guests —where they were from and how long they would be staying.

"I'll tell you later," Jed said. "They're in a hurry. I need the buggy."

Jed relished driving the hotel buggy. It made him feel rich and important, but today was different. Today he wished he was somewhere else, anywhere else than putting the harness on Eliminator and hooking up the buggy. As Jed drove the buggy around to the front of the hotel, he heard Wesley shout, "Praise God! My sister is marrying Jed the farmer!"

"Your chariot awaits, Wesley," Lydia shouted as she jumped in the buggy next to Jed. "Climb in and take your rightful place as matchmaker."

In a regal manner, Wesley bowed to an unseen crowd and climbed aboard. As the trio rode past the business district of town, Wesley went from shouting to muttering: "I'm happy. Lydia's happy. The farmer's happy. We all are happy. Praise God."

As they reached the outskirts of Rooster Creek, where the leaves on the trees in the foothills had changed from green to yellow, orange, and red, Jed took no delight in the scenery. Lydia could see by his grim face and the set of his jaw that he was anxious and distressed. When her shoulder touched his as the buggy bounced along, he moved ever farther away and tapped the reins for Eliminator to go at a faster pace.

To Jed, it was near miraculous that they had not seen anyone else on the road. Each mile away from the Rigby Hotel and Rooster Creek was welcomed as a gift and a chance to reclaim his life. *If Wesley stops his chanting within the hour, I can get the brother and sister to the railroad station in time to catch the ten o'clock train. If they need their bags, I'll go back to the hotel alone to get them.* For the first time since Wesley's outburst, Jed believed the whole thing would blow over. No one would know about his night with Lydia. He would marry Matilda on Saturday, and no one would be the wiser.

With some degree of calm and a smile on his face, Jed edged closer to Lydia. She was pleasantly surprised and relieved by the gesture. As Wesley sang, "Here comes the bride, with her handsome farmer at her side," Jed and Lydia laughed. Away from the danger of anyone who might hear him, Wesley's words were silly and entertaining. Another half mile, and they would cross the bridge and enter the Geneva Resort.

For reasons even Lydia didn't fully understand, she took out the pins that held her elaborate braid, allowing the glossy tendrils to cascade down her shoulders and onto the seat of the buggy. The early autumn wind, seeing its chance for some fun, blew great gusts of air, causing Lydia's silky strands to brush against the men on either side of her. Jed turned to look and could not take his eyes off Lydia. Lydia with hair pinned up was beautiful, but Lydia with hair unbound and blowing around her was glorious.

"Faster boy, faster!" Jed said to Eliminator. "Show Lydia you could win that Kentucky Derby."

The proud horse liked nothing better than to run. As Eliminator quickened his pace, Lydia's hair flew high above her head and whipped from side to side, tickling the men's faces. Wesley sang into the rushing wind, "The farmer had a wife. The farmer had a wife. High over the barrio, the farmer had a wife." Then lowering his voice to a deep bass, he added, "And the farmer's name is Jed."

Jed tapped the horse again, and Eliminator ran faster.

Wesley stopped singing and, in a stricken voice, shouted, "Slow down!"

"Calm down, Wesley," Lydia said. She put her arm in Jed's and nestled closer to him, her hair wrapping around the two of them like a blanket.

Wesley's face was white as a ghost. He clung to the edge of the buggy with one hand on the front and the other on the side. "Slow down!" he shrieked as Jed pushed Eliminator ever faster. The scenery flew past, blurring like a watercolor painting as the horse galloped closer and closer to the bridge. It was not until Eliminator slipped on the bridge, slick with morning dew, that Jed pulled up on the reins. He was too late. In an instant, Jed, Lydia, and Wesley were tossed from the buggy into the swirling water below.

5

ACCIDENT AT THE BRIDGE

Gasping for air and flailing his arms against the rushing water, Jed was the first to surface. Using the strength of his muscular frame, he swam against the raging current to reach the riverbank. With both hands, he frantically swept water from his eyes to see downriver as he shouted, "Lydia!" He saw Wesley bob up and down, splashing his arms wildly against the current. Jed pushed off from the bank, intending to swim to Wesley, but the current swept him off his feet and tumbled him against the rocks. He climbed back up on the riverbank and ran downstream to Wesley, who was being swept farther away. When he was within reaching distance, Jed grabbed hold of Wesley's twisting leg and pulled him to the bank.

"Lydia, where are you?" Jed called, his voice muffled by the sound of the roaring river. Ever more desperate, he shouted, "Lydia, answer!" There was no reply. About a half mile from where the buggy tipped over on the bridge, Jed finally spotted Lydia lying facedown in an eddy of the river. He jumped in the water and swam to her. He scooped her limp body into his arms and pulled her to the riverbank.

She was not moving as Jed laid her on the rocky shoreline. He tried to revive Lydia by pushing on her chest and turning her over and thumping on her back, but nothing worked. Tears flowed down his already wet face as he looked heavenward. "Oh, dear God, bring her back to life. Help her breathe."

She was gone.

When Wesley saw Jed's despair, he kneeled beside Lydia's body and wept, his scrawny frame shaking with emotion. "She's dead. My poor sister Lydia is dead," he moaned before shouting, "Arise like Lazarus! Come forth!" When Lydia didn't move, Wesley turned slowly to gaze at Jed. "You killed my sister," he hissed.

Jed shook his head, not in defiance of the accusation but in denial that beautiful Lydia was dead. He stood up and stepped backward. Tormented, he looked at the lifeless body. It was then he saw a bleeding bump on her head. "A rock must have knocked her out before she drowned," he said, turning to Wesley, who lay curled up on the ground like a potato bug. He was chanting, "You killed my sister. Like Cain killed Abel. You killed my sister."

As his accusation took root, Jed distanced himself from the crazed brother and paced back and forth between the trees that lined the riverbank. "Breathe, Lydia, breathe," he said in anguish. "Dear God, make her breathe." As the stillness of her body settled in, Jed felt helpless. He ran back to the bridge, looking in every direction for someone—anyone—who could help. Finding no one, he called out to the wind, "I didn't know the bridge was wet!"

Near the bridge, Jed saw Eliminator and hurried to unhitch the buggy. He mounted Eliminator and looked back at Wesley. "Stay with Lydia. I'll go for help."

"Don't go," Wesley pleaded. "Don't leave me with a corpse, the dried bones of a whitened sepulcher."

"I'll be back soon."

Jed rode like lightning through Rooster Creek toward the home of his friend Karl Ward. It took almost a half hour to reach his friend's stately home. Jed's legs gave way when he dismounted. Rising slowly from the ground, he promised himself that he wouldn't fall again. Jed ran up the path to the front porch. Holding on to the doorjamb for support, he knocked on the door.

"Oh my laws! Is that you, Jed?" Karl's mother exclaimed as she opened the door.

"Come in and sit by the stove and get warm before you faint. You look white as a ghost. Good heavens!"

Jed made no move to enter the house. "I'll wait here. Is Karl home?"

"He arrived last night excited to be your best man. You are a lucky man to be marrying Matilda Robinson. Wish Karl could find a woman like her."

"I don't have time to talk," Jed said with desperation in his voice. "Please get Karl."

"I'll fetch him right away but come inside. You're cold and wet. I'll grab a towel and a shirt while you stand by the stove." Karl's mother moved away from the front door, saying as she hurried down the hall, "Come in. I'll get Karl. I'm about to start breakfast."

Jed reluctantly entered the home and stood just inside the doorway.

When Karl appeared, he took one look at his friend's appearance and asked, "What happened to you? You look like a drowned rat."

"Here. Take this towel," Mrs. Ward said, offering the towel to Jed. "Dry yourself."

Jed took the towel.

"What's going on, Jed?" Karl asked.

"Here's a shirt," Mrs. Ward said. "Put it on, or you'll catch pneumonia before you have a chance to wed Matilda."

"I don't have time," Jed said.

"Nonsense. You take that wet shirt off and put the dry one on."

Jed tried to unbutton his shirt, but with frozen, shaking fingers, he couldn't. Giving up on the buttons, he pulled the wet shirt over his head and put on the dry one.

"Karl, can we talk in private? Outside?"

A few minutes later as they stood on the front porch, Karl said again, "Jed, tell me what's going on?"

"There was an accident. She drowned out at the bridge. The buggy slipped. We were tossed in the river."

"Who drowned? Who was tossed in the river?"

"All three of us."

"Why did you come to me and not Sheriff Thurston?"

"It's complicated."

"Complicated?" Karl asked.

"What's with all the questions?" Jed said. "Get your horse. Go with me to Sheriff Thurston's house."

"I'll hook up the buggy, and you can ride with me and fill me in."

Minutes later, as the two friends sat in the buggy, Jed pled with Karl to make the horse gallop. Karl refused, claiming a trot was plenty fast on roads still slick with morning dew. Over the sound of clopping horse hooves and wheels bumping against the rocky path, Jed said, "I need your...you know? When I talk to Sheriff Thurston."

"You're not making any sense," Karl said.

"I'm not good at... We can't all be... Listen."

"I am listening. Tell me what happened."

"Well, there was the awful accident, but the stuff about marriage that put us on the slippery bridge is not my fault. He's the cause of this mess."

"Come on, Jed," Karl said gently. "You're talking to your old friend. Start at the beginning and tell me what happened."

By now, the young friends had passed the Star Flour Mill and were entering Old Mill Lane. Jed calmed a bit as they rode on the familiar lane that ran parallel to the flowing stream touched by hanging tree limbs. As he spoke, his voice sounded stronger. "They..."

"Who's they?" Karl asked.

"I told you already. The brother and sister. Since you went off to college, I've been working as the night clerk at the Rigby Hotel. Normally, nothing happens after midnight. I heard the door open, and it was a photographer. He was an ornery cuss, but I gave him a room anyway. Then this couple I was telling you about came through the door. I checked them in. I thought the guy was the girl's dad. He was mangy looking. Looked like he was starving. I couldn't see her very well in the shadowy room, but I could tell that she was pretty."

"Okay, so you checked them in. Then what happened?"

"I'm trying to tell you. After I checked them in, they went upstairs. I thought that was that. About an hour later, the sister came downstairs telling me her brother snored, and she couldn't sleep. I told her to sleep on the couch in the lobby. I should've kicked her out. Nothing would've—"

"Did she sleep on the couch?"

"Not for very long."

"How long was she down there with you?"

"She didn't come down until after midnight. She wasn't there too long—just until morning."

"You spent the night together." It wasn't a question. The hint of chastisement in Karl's tone chafed Jed.

"Not the whole night. She told me her brother sent her down to the lobby because I was a farmer, and he wanted her to marry a farmer. The crazy coot said God told him she was to marry me."

Karl pulled up on the reins to stop the horse. "You're marrying Matilda on Saturday, and you spent the night with a strange woman. Did anything happen?"

"Of course stuff happened."

"What?"

"We talked and stuff like that."

"No loving stuff."

"Course not. Like you said, I'm engaged to Matilda." Jed looked away from Karl's hard stare and mumbled, "Maybe just one kiss, and I hugged her once, but that was when we were saying goodbye. We've got to hurry to Sheriff Thurston's house. Prod the horse."

"I'm not going anywhere until I get the rest of the story," Karl said. "Go on."

"When she told me why she came downstairs, I laughed my head off and told her she was on a wild goose chase because I was getting married in a few days. She was really easy to talk to. Made me wish I wasn't marrying Matilda." Then, grabbing Karl's arm, Jed said, "She was a real beauty. I know you want to marry a beautiful woman. I wanted to introduce Lydia to you."

"Oh boy, Jed. You are really something! So what else happened?"

"Lydia said she didn't want any part of breaking Matilda's heart. She told me that it didn't make sense for us to be together. I knew she was right, but..." Jed's voice trailed off into silence.

"So how did you end up at the bridge?" Karl asked, snapping Jed's thoughts back from his complicated feelings about the predicament at hand.

"In the morning, the brother came down to the lobby. He thought we were going to wed. He went out to Main Street and yelled in a high-pitch voice that Lydia and I were getting married. Neither of us could calm him."

"So you had to get him out of there."

"Yeah." Jed sighed, grateful Karl was following the story. "I was taking them to the Geneva Resort, but I was going too fast when we got to the bridge. And now...she's gone."

The friends sat in silence for a few moments as the mention of death hung in the air.

It was not until they moved on to Main Street that Jed spoke again. "We'll be at Sheriff Thurston's house in a minute. Karl, you've got to help me." Seeing his friend hesitate, Jed said, "There's more I need to say before we get to Thurston's. I want you to hear the whole story, so you'll know why I need your help."

"First, I have some questions," Karl said. "For starters, what about the brother? Where's he?"

"With Lydia at the bridge," Jed said.

"You left him alone with his sister's body?" Karl asked in disbelief.

"I want you to back me up when I tell the sheriff that I never talked to the brother and sister after I checked them into the hotel until this morning when they asked me to take them on a short sightseeing ride in the country."

"According to what you just told me, that's not true."

"I know, but that's what I'm going to tell the sheriff."

"Come on, Jed. Somebody must know about you and the woman talking about getting married."

"There was a photographer," Jed mused, "but he left on the early morning train for California. He'll never come back here. He hates Rooster Creek."

"What about the brother? You said he was in on it."

"He's the craziest man I've ever seen. Nobody will listen to a word he says. The photographer took a picture of Lydia and me. He developed it upstairs in the hotel. As he was handing the photograph to me, he jokingly said, 'Looks like a wedding picture.' The crazy brother heard and started shouting that Lydia and I were getting married."

"Where's the photographer?" Karl asked, struggling to keep up with Jed's twisting tale.

"Like I told you, he caught the morning train. I'll never hear from him again."

Karl shook his head. "The brother's not the crazy one."

"Are you calling me crazy?" Jed asked. "I'm telling you what happened."

"I don't know how I can help," Karl said. "Did anyone besides the photographer hear the brother shout that you and Lydia were getting married?"

"I don't think so. We drove out of Rooster Creek early. Both brother and sister planned to leave town on the ten o'clock train. After we calmed the brother down at the Geneva Resort, I was going to drive them to the train station. The whole thing would have blown over if there had been no accident."

"You have to tell the truth," Karl said. "A woman is dead!"

"I can't tell the truth," Jed exclaimed. "It would wreck everything with Matilda. It would ruin my life. If I tell the truth, everyone will say, 'Jed Dawson is worse than his drunk father. Spends the night in the hotel with some floozy who came in on the train, and by morning, they decided to get married.' You've got to help me. You're smarter than me. Don't turn your back on me now."

Karl gritted his teeth. "You want me to lie for you?" His words were quiet and angry. "You want me to tell Sheriff Thurston that the brother and sister are strangers, and you were just giving them a ride? Tell the truth. People will get over it. Matilda will know that you meant no harm. Tell the truth!"

"I can't. I just can't."

"The brother will tell the truth as he sees it, and when he does, it will be tough on you and Matilda."

"If you won't help me, then drop me off and ride home," Jed said. "I'm going to tell Sheriff Thurston that the brother and sister stayed in the Rigby Hotel and asked me to give them a sightseeing ride in the buggy."

"Jed, a woman died, and all you care about is how you are going to look to the townsfolk."

"I care about Lydia," Jed said. "She had lots of problems, and I wanted to help. Now she's gone. I'm willing to admit that I was driving the buggy when she died, but don't accuse me of not caring about her death." With that, Jed pulled out his handkerchief and wiped his eyes. Between sobs, he said, "I can't face people all over town talking about me like I'm my dad."

6

THE LIE

K arl tied his horse to the sheriff's fencepost and walked with Jed up the lane to the front porch. Neither seemed in a hurry, though the urgency was great. Jed was afraid of Sheriff Walter Thurston in the best of times. Almost all the folks in Rooster Creek felt the same. Even Karl was afraid, though he would never admit it.

"The sheriff may not be home," Jed said as they stood on the porch. "It's after nine."

"If my dad were here, he'd tell you that the lazy sheriff is still in bed."

Karl pounded on the door as if hoping to wake the sleeping lawman. Glancing at the hunched shoulders of his childhood friend, it was as if Karl were seeing again the boy who'd come to his bedroom window, bony back curved, making himself smaller to hide from the dark eyes of his drunken father. The two friends never spoke on those nights. Karl would open the window, and Jed would crawl in and nestle down on the pile of extra blankets kept for such occasions.

"This had better be important," Sheriff Thurston said as he threw the door wide open. "I'm eating breakfast, and oatmeal's not good when it's cold. Make it quick." He stood in the doorway, one hand on his hip in a gesture of disgust and the other stroking the left side of his handlebar mustache. He waited for Karl or Jed to speak. Jed was silent as a tomb and stared at his shoes. Karl, without the slightest tremor in his voice, spoke boldly on Jed's behalf.

"There's been an accident at the bridge," Karl said. "Jed was taking two strangers, a brother and his sister, to the resort to see the sites before they caught the morning train to California. They were guests at the Rigby Hotel. The buggy slipped on the bridge. The woman drowned. The brother is at the river with her body."

Karl looked at Jed, and their eyes met. Karl was filled with regret for having told a lie, but Jed was pleased and bit his lip, trying not to smile.

Sheriff Thurston pulled a pine nut from his pocket, cracked it open with his teeth, tossed it into his mouth, and said, laboring on each word, "Let me get this straight. Jed was working last night as the night clerk at Fred Rigby's. Two people checked in. In the morning, he gave them a joyride. The buggy went off the bridge, and a woman drowned."

"That's the way Jed explained it to me, Sheriff," Karl said.

"It'll take me a few minutes to hitch up the buggy."

"You can ride in mine," Karl insisted.

The sheriff laughed and crunched another pine nut. "That old rig wouldn't make it to the river. It's about time your old man bought a new one. That thing's a wreck." He crunched another pine nut as if to emphasize his disdain for the buggy and its owner.

Unable to restrain himself, even in the presence of an authority figure, Karl said, "It's your buggy I'm worried about."

The sheriff shifted from one foot to the other as if he had been hit.

Sheriff Thurston left Jed and Karl standing on the porch. He needed to telephone his deputy, Elmer Top.

"Elmer, did you get to the office on time today? I can't abide a tardy deputy. Now write this down. Phone Seth and tell him there's a dead body at the bridge. Have him bring the wagon. I'll meet him there. Stay by the phone. I'll call if we need backup. Now repeat that back to me."

Sheriff Thurston listened as the dim-witted deputy slowly repeated his message. He then flipped a pine nut in his mouth, followed by a mouthful of cold oatmeal that tasted more like glue than anything else. He grabbed his coat and then headed to the barn, where he harnessed his horse and hitched up the buggy.

"I'll lead the way," the sheriff yelled over his shoulder. "Try to keep up."

"That man's insufferable. No matter what happened at the bridge, I'd never ride with the sheriff," Karl murmured as he and Jed ran down the lane and jumped in the Ward buggy.

As he drove to the bridge, Sheriff Thurston's thoughts turned to recent tragedies he'd encountered—the deaths of the three Heath children in a tragic house fire, the snow slide up Rooster Creek Canyon that wiped out a mining camp, and the Smedley boy killed by a rattlesnake bite. *It is a difficult job being sheriff. Not just anyone can do it.*

In the buggy behind Sheriff Thurston, Jed talked nonstop about Karl's true friendship. Karl, lost in regret, did not hear a word.

As the buggies approached the bridge, Jed called over to Sheriff Thurston. "The brother and sister are near the river bend. I can see them."

Once they'd stopped, the men stepped out of the buggies and ran to the bend. They saw Wesley on the ground, propping up his sister's body and braiding her hair. Wesley didn't look up as the men approached. He was too busy deftly arranging the braids in a concentric circle atop Lydia's head.

"Lydia wouldn't want you to see her with her hair down," Wesley said. "It's unbecoming for a Christian woman." Wesley gently laid her body down on the ground and asked the men to bow their heads as he prayed. "Dear God, into thy hands I commend the Christian Lydia."

In unison, they said, "Amen."

The solemnity of the amen chorus ended all too quickly.

"You left me in the shadow of death with a corpse for comfort," Wesley said, pointing a bony finger at Jed. "Lydia was going to be your wife. She was your Eve. Why didn't you stay with her and let me go for help?"

The sheriff looked perplexed. Fighting against self-inflicted guilt and better judgment, Karl said, "Nonsense! You're her brother. Jed saved your life. Jed did all he could for you, and then he went for help. You should thank him."

Wesley arose, phoenix-like in indigent majesty. "What's going on here? Has heaven turned a blind eye?" Looking at Sheriff Thurston, he asked, "Are you a sheriff?"

"Been the sheriff in Rooster Creek ever since Mr. Ward was elected mayor. Mayor says I'm like Wyatt Earp."

"Jed was going to marry my sister," Wesley told him in a high-pitched voice. "He was pushing his horse to go faster. I told him to slow down. The wheels of the buggy went off the bridge. Jed killed my sister like Cain killed Abel. He killed the very woman he wanted to marry."

Sheriff Thurston threw another pine nut in his mouth. "You sound like a lunatic. Just tell me what happened."

In an even higher shrill, Wesley shouted, "Arrest that man! Jed Dawson killed my sister!"

"Why is he talking this way?" Sheriff Thurston asked, turning to look at Jed. "Were you planning to marry his sister?"

"I'm marrying your niece Matilda Robinson on Saturday. Why would I ask anyone else to marry me? I love Matilda."

The sheriff turned back to look at Wesley. "That man called you Jed. Sure sounds like he knows you."

Karl could see Jed was in a tough position. To prevent him from saying something foolish, he interjected. "The brother knows his name because he asked Jed to take him and his sister to the Geneva Resort."

"That's not true!" Wesley shouted.

"Are you calling me a liar?" Jed shot back. "I wasn't going to marry your sister. I'm marrying Matilda Robinson on Saturday. You're crazy!"

"What are you trying to do?" the sheriff asked, somewhat amused, as he looked at Wesley. "I've known Jed Dawson for years. I watched him play the championship basketball game against Lehi High School. He made the winning shot. And you? You probably don't even play basketball. You're a drifter. Are you looking for a payoff of some kind?"

"I don't want a payoff," Wesley growled. "I want the truth." He lunged at Jed and grabbed his arm. "Tell the truth!" he screamed. "Show the sheriff the photograph! If you won't, I will. I'll tell everyone in this town that you were going to marry my sister and that you killed her."

"What photograph? There's no photograph." Jed sneered as he easily broke free from Wesley's grasp.

Sheriff Thurston stepped between the two men and shoved Wesley to the ground, threatening to handcuff him if he didn't stop his rantings. "The whole thing's a tragedy," the sheriff said to Jed. "I'm sorry it happened just a few days before your wedding. The undertaker will be here soon to pick up the body. We'll hold a funeral, and then this feller—Wesley is it?—can be on his way."

"The undertaker is here," Karl said. "He's approaching the bridge."

Seth Warenski was Rooster Creek's one and only undertaker. He inherited the role from his father, who inherited it from his father. As much as his vocation confronted him with death on a regular basis, Seth never got used to it. Townsfolk thought Warenski was a wonderful undertaker but unusually awkward, often stumbling over a dirt clod or rock during a burial service. Yet they talked of him as the kindest, tallest man in town—their own Abraham Lincoln. Seth discounted their compliments but inwardly took pride in knowing people had such confidence in him and his integrity.

As Seth pulled the wagon closer to where the men stood, he could see the body of a woman on the ground. He jumped down from his wagon and hurried toward the mournful scene. The men moved back to give him room.

"Drowned?" Seth asked, even though he already knew the cause of death. But he knew it comforted the bereaved to hear him speak as he examined the deceased.

"The buggy slipped on the bridge and tossed her and her brother into the river," Sheriff Thurston said. "Jed saved the brother but couldn't save his sister. As far as I can tell, she drowned."

Tears of sympathy pooled in Seth's eyes and spilled down his cheeks as he tenderly lifted Lydia's head off the ground. "Bad bump on her head too, but I don't think that killed her—a drowning all right." He put his fingers on her wrist and shook his head. He put his ear close to her mouth to listen for breath. There was none. Still kneeling, he looked up and said in a deep soft voice, "She's gone." The undertaker stood up and looked down at the body from his great height. He wiped his nose with his handkerchief, shook his head, and whispered, "Such a beautiful woman. So young too."

After pausing for a stretch, Seth asked, "Can two or three of you give me a hand? Let's get her body over to the wagon." Karl moved forward to assist as did Wesley. Jed took a step backward.

The three men carried Lydia's limp body to the wagon and gently laid her in the back.

"She was a beauty," Sheriff Thurston whispered to the undertaker. "Don't see the likes of her in Rooster Creek. I wouldn't blame Jed if he had wanted to marry her. My niece Matilda is the woman you take home to meet your mother. This beauty would turn the head of every man in town."

Seth carefully pulled a canvas tarp over Lydia's body. When the tarp was pulled up to her neck, he bent down and kissed her forehead. With great care, he pulled the tarp over her face.

Watching the body being covered by the tarp, Karl allowed himself to feel anguish for the first time that morning—to feel deep remorse for the death of a woman and for his lie. He glanced at Jed and hoped his friend felt the same. He couldn't tell. Jed's hands covered his face.

The sheriff instructed Wesley to sit next to the undertaker on the buckboard. Contrary to his earlier behavior, Wesley complied.

Seth spoke slowly and carefully to Wesley. "I know this is difficult for you. Tomorrow will be better. There's always a bright day ahead. Then you can tell me about—"

"Tell you?" Wesley interrupted. "Why would I tell a gravedigger anything? But I will tell you that man right there—Jed Dawson—is a liar. He'll pay the price. 'An eye for an eye,' just like Moses said."

Karl stood away from the others, shaking his head ever so slightly. The hole he'd dug with Jed was getting dangerously deep and filling with quicksand. Guilt crept in as his mind raced to questions that had no answers: *Where was the photograph? Would Wesley stay in Rooster Creek, telling his story of Jed and the accident?*

The sheriff, opting for a friendlier stance now that Wesley was seated in the wagon, said, "If Seth approves, we will hold a funeral tomorrow for your sister. After the funeral, I'll give you a train ticket so you can move along."

Wesley looked straight ahead and said nothing. All he could think of was revenge. Seth gave the signal for his horse to move. The wagon crossed the bridge and headed back to Rooster Creek with the undertaker and Wesley in the front and Lydia bound in a tarp in the back.

"You fellers better go home," the sheriff said to Karl and Jed. The sheriff threw another pine nut in his mouth, breaking it open with his teeth, spitting out the shell, and chomping down. "That is if that rig of old man Ward's doesn't break down before you get there." He laughed at his joke.

Karl didn't flinch. The verbal war between the Wards and Thurstons was secondary to the problems that lay ahead.

When Jed and Karl pulled away, the sheriff walked to the bridge to watch the swirling white water. Returning to his buggy, he smiled as his mind turned to a pleasant thought—taking his wife for her morning walk.

7

LYDIA

"Take me to the hotel," Jed said to Karl. "I need to pick up something."

Karl felt lightheaded. He'd had enough for one day and wanted to go home. He mostly wanted to get away from Jed.

"Come on, Jed. Nothing more. I want to go home," Karl said. "I need to think."

"It won't take long. Take me to the hotel."

Against his better judgment, Karl turned the horse and buggy around and went down Main Street to the Rigby Hotel. Jed jumped out of the buggy and ran to open the door.

"Mrs. Rigby, are you here?" he called. "Mrs. Rigby?" When she didn't answer, he motioned for Karl to come inside. Jed stepped ever so softly on the wood-planked floor. Karl watched as he pulled a Montgomery Ward catalog from under a cushion on the couch, walked to the desk, and opened the top drawer. He watched him carefully take something from the drawer, place it inside the catalog, and put the catalog under his arm. He then gestured for Karl to follow him. They walked out of the hotel lobby into broad daylight unnoticed.

Karl said nothing about the catalog Jed held under his arm as they sat in the buggy. He didn't want to know. He was thinking of the lies, the dead woman, and her brother saying, "An eye for an eye." Karl knew what the biblical phrase meant, but he did not know how the brother would pull it off.

As they drove through Old Mill Lane, Jed gripped Karl's hand. "Pull up on the reins."

"Not now," Karl said. "We're going home."

"I want to show you the photograph."

The young men alighted from the buggy and walked to the privacy of a grove of trees. Jed carefully lifted the photograph from the catalog.

Karl purposely looked in the other direction. "Don't show me. I already know too much. Put it away, take it home, and destroy it."

"Wasn't Lydia the most beautiful woman you've ever seen?" Jed said, shoving the photograph at him. "How would it have been to be married to her?"

Karl involuntarily glanced at the photograph and saw the image of a woman as a bride and Jed as the groom, evidence that Wesley had told the truth. With his head hanging as low as the tree limbs that licked the rushing stream, Karl climbed back in the buggy. He gave a signal for the horse to move forward. Jed caught up, jumped in, and tried to convince Karl it was not a wedding photograph.

"Get rid of it," Karl said. "The photograph's evidence you proposed to Lydia. Did you lie about that too?"

"I told the truth. We talked about being together, but we knew there was no way." Jed stared at the photograph. "I can't throw this away. Don't you see, Karl? Lydia will always be the woman I—"

"You lied to Sheriff Thurston. No! *We* told a lie to Sheriff Thurston. We claimed you hardly knew Wesley and Lydia. That's perjury. We can be thrown in jail for perjury. Lydia's gone. Her brother will tell his story to anyone who will listen. We are in real trouble."

"Nobody will believe that drifter. Sheriff Thurston already thinks he's crazy."

"Don't be too sure," Karl said. "I think of myself as a man of integrity. I'm a law student and have sworn to uphold the law. I'd like to be that man again. I'm begging you. Let's go back to the bridge and find Sheriff Thurston. He's probably still there trying to figure out how to get the Rigby buggy upright. Let's tell him the truth."

"You think you're so good, 'man of integrity' and all that rot, but what if it had been you?"

Jed and Karl sat in heated silence as they rode up Alpine Road. When Karl stopped in front of Jed's house, Jed looked at him and said, "Try to see this through my eyes. You left Rooster Creek for law school in Vegas. I would like to leave this place too. I want to find a new life. I don't want to be a chicken farmer, but I have no chance of ever leaving this town. Matilda and I will live out our days in Rooster Creek. Don't ask me to destroy the photograph. It's my link to a beautiful woman. I kissed her and wondered what life might have been if I had met her before Matilda. I'll keep the photograph where no one will find it."

The two friends stared at each other. Karl knew Jed desperately wanted his approval, something he could not give. Jed sighed and got out of the buggy. He stood in the road, looking at Karl, who wouldn't meet his gaze. Instead, he pulled on the reins and drove away,

IN SOME STRANGE SENSE, it was the same for Seth Warenski and Wesley Birch. For the first few miles, Seth and Wesley looked straight ahead. Wesley's mind was whirling with betrayal and being left without recourse. Seth was offering a silent prayer, asking the Lord to help him say the right words to comfort the bereaved stranger.

As awkward as one man could speak to another, Seth blurted out, "Look, I don't really know what's going on."

"A bunch of lies is what's going on," Wesley said. "My sister and I came to town on the train last night from Nebraska. We went to the hotel, and Jed checked us in. He fooled me into thinking he was a good man. He says nothing happened last night and that he doesn't know Lydia. He said that a wedding photograph was never taken, and he never intended to marry my sister. It's a lie."

For the first time Wesley looked at Seth and asked, "Do you believe me? No one at the bridge believed me."

Seth paused long enough for Wesley to ask again.

"You believe me? The sheriff doesn't believe me. That man with Jed doesn't believe me, but they weren't in the hotel. I was."

"I've known Jed Dawson all his life," Seth said slowly. "He comes from a troubled home, but he has risen above his father. He's an honest man, well respected in town. But I can't see why you would make this up. Let me think on it."

Wesley looked down at the floorboard and shook his head back and forth a half dozen times as Seth asked himself, *Did Jed ask a woman he had known for only a few hours to marry him? Doesn't sound like the Jed I know, but why would this stranger make up such a tale?*

Seth didn't know how to respond to Wesley. Maybe he would know later. In his undertaker voice, he repeated words that often comforted the bereaved: "There is no trial in life greater than the passing of a loved one. If all people could live life to old age and experience all the joy of living, it would be better. Sadly, death claims even the young and beautiful—like your sister."

"Could you speak louder?" Wesley said. "I didn't hear a word you said."

Seth cringed. Whenever he tried to comfort the bereaved, his voice softened to a soothing, almost inaudible tone. As much as he tried, his voice never matched his great height.

"Since I can't hear you, I'll tell you something," Wesley said. "This place you call Rooster Creek is nothing more than Sodom and Gomorrah. That man you call the sheriff is a sinner. That other man, the short guy, is a liar. The worst is Jed Dawson. Like a sheep in wolf's clothing, he looked like a good man—a farmer—an answer to my prayers. He is the devil in disguise—Judas the traitor."

"Rooster Creek is a good town," Seth said. "Fine people live here. None perfect, but many who try to be. Have some mercy, some forgiveness. It makes life easier."

"Forgiveness. Ha! I'll never forgive Jed Dawson. Moses had it right. 'An eye for an eye.' If it takes the rest of my life, I'll make sure that man pays for killing my sister."

The undertaker had seen hate before but never so up close and raw. For the first time in his life, Seth felt fear. He looked at the small, bony man seated next to him and wondered what evil he was capable of conceiving. As the slow-moving horse made its way to the mortuary, Seth didn't try to share additional words of comfort. He was too concerned about his shaking hands and hoped Wesley hadn't noticed.

When they arrived at the mortuary, Seth walked around to the back of the wagon to retrieve the body. Wesley followed. Without saying a word, they carried Lydia's body up the front stairs and into the mortuary—Seth going backward with hands under her arms and Wesley holding her ankles. They carefully laid the body on the examination table. Wesley stood back as Seth removed the canvas. Seeing his sister in death's grip, Wesley collapsed into a chair, putting his elbows on his thighs, and cradling his head in his hands.

"Are you all right?" Seth asked.

Wesley raised his head and looked at Seth without answering. Although Seth wished he could take the stranger in his arms and comfort his tortured soul, fear prevented the close encounter.

"I'll get a clean dress for your sister from the closet," he said. "I have a wardrobe to choose from. Folks in Rooster Creek never throw away their clothes. They bring them to me. I mend and iron them and get them ready for burial. I'll be just a moment. I'll bring a washcloth to clean up your sister and a comb for her hair."

At the mention of Lydia's hair, Wesley stood up. "I'll fix her hair.

Mother would have wanted it that way. Bring me a pan of water, a towel, and a comb."

Seth nodded and started gathering the items. When he returned, he set them down on the table next to Lydia. "I'll leave you two alone for a while."

Fifteen minutes later, Wesley called out, "You can come back now."

"Her hair looks beautiful," Seth said. "Your mother would be pleased."

"My mother used to brush Lydia's hair hour after hour," Wesley said, sitting down and thinking of days gone by. "I listened to the words my mother said as she brushed her hair. She taught Lydia how to speak German and how to be a lady. They were happy."

Wesley put his hand on the back of his head to massage his neck and took a deep breath before saying, "When Mother died two years ago, the light went out of Lydia's life. She was always on the verge of tears. I can almost rejoice in knowing she is once again with Mother and happy. But in her death, *my* happiness is gone."

"I'm sure you miss your mother too."

"Father died in the same accident."

"That's too much for anyone to handle. And now your sister's death."

Seth took out a handkerchief and wiped his eyes. As the men stared at Lydia, Seth noticed a small locket dangling from her neck. He lifted Lydia's head, removed the locket and chain, and handed it to Wesley. "You'll be wanting this," he said.

Wesley took the locket and chain and put them around his neck.

"Wesley, I don't know you very well, but I'd like to consider you a friend," Seth said, hoping to convince the strange man that he was on his side.

For the first time since the tragic accident, Wesley felt comfort. He nodded without making eye contact.

"I'll prepare your sister for burial," Seth said. "We'll hold her funeral tomorrow at noon. You can sleep in the mortuary tonight."

"Sleep? How could I sleep when justice has not received her due? Jed Dawson still moves about."

Again, a wave of fear swept over Seth. With hands shaking violently, he led Wesley down the hall to the guest room. When Seth opened the door to the room, Wesley pushed past him, collapsed on the mattress, and slept.

Seth had planned to say, "I'll be right back with food," but never had the chance.

Seth did not linger in the guest room. He wanted to lock the door and throw away the key. He feared the small man. Never had he felt such deep sorrow for a man or such great fear, but the funeral was tomorrow, and his emotions needed to be kept in check.

There was dried blood on Lydia's forehead to wash up. Seth was in his element as he handled a tin basin of warm water, bar of soap, washcloth, towel, and the freshly ironed yellow cotton dress. Ever so gently, he wet Lydia's forehead until the clotted dark blood turned a crimson red, then pale pink, before washing away. As he carefully washed near her hairline, he saw the left eyebrow move. He jumped back, splashing water all over himself and the carpet. He folded his arms, cocked his head, and stared at Lydia's face. *I'm spooking myself. Get a grip. You've done this a hundred times.*

As he washed the right arm, the left eyebrow moved again. Seth reached for Lydia's wrist to feel for a pulse. Nothing. *What's the matter with me? I'd better stop this and call Thurston right away. I'm spooking myself with a corpse in front of me and a crazy man down the hall.* As he moved toward the telephone, Seth heard a slight moan, which caused his body to stiffen as his senses tingled to full attention. Something was going on—something he'd only heard about at church. He moved closer to the body to witness a miracle in the making. There was life in the still body! He felt for a pulse again and detected the slight rushing of pumping blood. He saw Lydia's right knee bend ever so slightly.

He bent over the body and whispered, "Lydia, can you hear me?"

Lydia's nod was almost imperceptible. Seth reverently hovered nearby with tears streaming down his cheeks before hurrying down the hall to the faucet to pour a glass of water. He rushed back to Lydia, put his hand behind her neck, and gently raised her head.

"How do you feel?" he asked as he pressed the glass lightly against her lips. She opened her mouth and swallowed. She tried to speak, but her voice was raspy, and her words garbled.

She grimaced as if the act of speaking was physically painful, yet she persisted. "Is Frank here? Did he do this to me?"

"I don't know who Frank is," Seth replied. "He's not here. He has never been here."

"Where am I? Where's Wesley? Where's Jed?"

Lydia tried to stand, but Seth cautioned her.

"You're weak. Sit on the side of the table if you must, but don't stand up. You've been in a terrible accident at the bridge. I'm the undertaker. I brought you to the mortuary thinking you were dead."

"An accident?" Lydia asked, her voice still raspy and slurred.

"Do you remember coming to Rooster Creek?"

"Wesley and I came on a train. We got off at Rooster Creek. Wesley wanted me to marry a farmer. He made me go down to the hotel lobby and talk to Jed."

Seth listened patiently, slightly stunned as Lydia recovered her memories about Jed.

"I liked him. He kissed me. He hugged me. Wesley acted crazy and thought we were getting married. I should never have agreed to let the photographer take a picture of me and Jed. Then there was the buggy. We were going too fast. I don't remember anything after that."

"The buggy slipped off the bridge," Seth continued for her. "You were thrown in the raging river. Jed saved your brother. When he found you, you were facedown in the river. I confirmed there was no life in you. There was no pulse, no breath. I brought you in my wagon to the mortuary." Wiping his eyes, Seth said, "Never in all my life have I seen such a thing. It's a miracle. I'll wake up Wesley and tell him. Then I'll telephone Sheriff Thurston, Jed, and Karl. This is too great a miracle to keep to myself. There has never been such a miracle as this in Rooster Creek."

Lydia's eyes filled with tears and, in a voice harsh with anguish, whispered, "Do I have to be alive? Living is too hard."

"You don't mean what you're saying," Seth said, taking Lydia's hand. "You're so young. Life will be good to you again. I promise."

Lydia shook her head. "I have nothing to live for."

"But you are young and beautiful," Seth countered.

"My beauty is nothing but a curse. Take Jed, for instance. Did he tell you the story of our romance?"

"He denied even knowing you except for checking you into the hotel and giving you a ride to the country," Seth said.

"Jed denied that we spent the night together and talked of marriage?"

"Yes. His friend Karl backed him up."

"Sorrow follows me like a shadow," Lydia said. "I'm a fool to think it could ever be otherwise, or that I was more to Jed than a one-night kiss."

"Your brother is asleep down the hall," Seth said. "I'll wake him. He'll want to be part of this miracle."

As Seth turned to walk out of the room, Lydia grabbed his arm. "Does Wesley think I'm dead?"

"He has been in absolute anguish. You should have heard him ranting and raving: 'Jed killed my sister. As Moses said, An eye for an eye.' Sheriff Thurston told him to stop saying such crazy things and threw him to the ground. It was an unforgettable scene. The first miracle today was getting Wesley to the mortuary. The second miracle is that you are alive! I'll get him."

"Don't tell Wesley that I am alive," Lydia said quickly. "I'm afraid of him."

Seth knew the feeling all too well, for he, too, was afraid of the small, bony man.

"He's crazy," Lydia said. "All that religious talk has made him a lunatic. Could you take me to the train station?"

"Where would you go?"

"It doesn't matter as long as I get away from Wesley and Frank."

"I would be glad to talk to Wesley on your behalf. I'm confident a new arrangement could be worked out so that you could be happy. Besides, you don't look old enough to live on your own. You could stay in Rooster Creek, and he could catch the train. You would be happy here. Townsfolk would help you get back on your feet."

"Like Jed Dawson?" Lydia asked. "This is not your problem; it's mine. I made it this far, and I want to catch the train. Will you help me?"

Seth began to protest, but before he really could, Lydia changed the subject.

"I must look a mess. Could you get me some soap and water? I need to clean up."

"Of course! When we thought you were dead, Wesley braided your hair."

Lydia smiled faintly for the first time.

8

THE PLAN

"You can't stay in the parlor," Seth said to Lydia. "Windows don't lie, and it's too early to pull the drapes. Wesley's in the guest room, so you can't go there. It wouldn't look good for you to go upstairs to my bedroom...and the only other room is down the hall, where I keep my burial supplies. The smell is horrible there, but you'll be safe from gawking eyes. The accident at the bridge is no doubt the talk in town. Townsfolk will want to see the beauty."

Without hesitating, Lydia swung her legs over the edge of the table. Seth stood close. She took his arm and slowly walked to the storage room. Seth opened the door and led her to a chair near the table where he mixed toxic potions.

"I'll leave the door slightly ajar. I'm going out to the barn to milk Buttercup. I'll be back in fifteen minutes."

"You have a cow?"

"Everyone in Rooster Creek has a cow. We're all farmers at heart."

"But there's only one rooster in town?"

"That's right! One rooster wakes up the whole town."

Lydia smiled.

Seth rushed out the backdoor, picked up the milk bucket, and walked at a fast clip to the barn. For most folks in Rooster Creek, it was a chore to milk cows, but not for Seth. Years ago, he figured out a perfect routine: put oats in a wooden trough for Buttercup's evening meal, pick up the three-legged stool, and squirt milk in the bucket held between his knees while Buttercup ate. But it wasn't his routine that brought Seth pleasure. The act of milking brought out his best thinking.

This afternoon he had much to think about—fear of Wesley, the predicament facing Lydia as she dealt with her fears of Wesley and someone named Frank, Sheriff Thurston swallowing Jed and Karl's lie, and the miracle of Lydia's rebirth. With so much to ponder, it was strange that Seth's mind fixed on a scene from *A Tale of Two Cities* by Charles Dickens. In the scene, a friend chooses to pose as the main character, who was sentenced to death. While the friend awaits execution, he says, "It is a far, far better thing that I do, than I have ever done."

Seth had always hoped someday, somehow, he could do a far greater thing than he had ever done. Comforting the bereaved was second nature to him. Some might say it was a far better thing. But to Seth, there had to be something more. Perhaps today his chance had come—a chance to do something for Lydia that was better than anything he had ever done before.

When the bucket was half-full of foaming, warm milk, Seth stopped milking. His mind was buzzing at a feverish pitch. *Wesley thinks she's dead—so do Jed, Karl, and the sheriff. What if they were never told about the miracle?* He looked across the barn to see if his two sixty-pound sacks of oats were still on the floor. *The sacks together equal the weight of Lydia. I could place them inside the coffin, then nail it shut and explain that Lydia's head injury continued to swell in an unusual grotesque manner, making a public viewing impossible. There could still be a funeral, a eulogy, and a burial. Yet if anyone found out I faked a burial—I'd be ruined. They would expect me to dig up every Tom, Dick, and Harry in the graveyard to make sure the bodies were there. I'd lose my mortician's license. Yet I could put Lydia on tonight's ten o'clock train headed for Vegas. She would have to be disguised, of course. So many issues to consider, but like the character from my favorite book, I would sacrifice myself for another. The biggest lie in the history of Rooster Creek would not be Jed's; it would be mine.*

Seth stood and, with bucket in hand, ran back to the mortuary. He dropped the bucket at the door and hurried down the hall to the guest room. Without opening the door, he could hear Wesley's heavy snoring and was grateful. He then went to the supply room and knocked softly.

"Is that you, Seth?" Lydia whispered.

Without any preamble or inquiry as to her well-being, Seth blurted out his plan. He was sorely disappointed when Lydia outright rejected it.

"My mother would never approve of anything so deceitful," she said. "I could never do it. What if someone found out? Wouldn't you go to jail?"

When Seth nodded, Lydia's eyes widened in disbelief. "You're willing to risk everything—even your mortuary—for me?"

As far as Seth was concerned, the plan was a done deal. He had only to convince its key player. "I've been accused of being a fool more than once. But the way I see this playing out, it is your opportunity to start anew. Wesley would not be with you to call the shots in your life. If Frank—whoever that is—ever came to Rooster Creek, everyone in town would tell him you died in an accident at the bridge. You never need to fear that man again. Can't you see, Lydia? This is the answer."

"How can you do this? You hardly know me," Lydia said as she looked into Seth's eyes.

"What's my purpose in life if not to help others? If I did nothing, my life would go on much the same. By helping you live a life without fear and sadness, my life will be better knowing I helped make that possible."

Lydia reached up and touched Seth's cheek ever so softly before whispering, "I'll do it."

"You'll need to change your name," Seth said. "I like the name Ann Golding. I read it once in a book and liked it ever since." Seth reached out his hands and rested them on Lydia's shoulders. "What do you think?"

"Ann Golding is my name."

"I imagine there is little chance that Frank will come to Rooster Creek, but we must not take any chances. When you get on the ten o'clock train, let's never meet or communicate in any way. I don't want to be the one who gives away your freedom or safety."

Lydia nodded. But then, quite suddenly, she gasped. "What about Jed?"

"It is best for both of you if he never knows. He'll go ahead with his wedding on Saturday to Matilda Robinson. It will be a gala event. Everyone in town is invited."

Lydia shrugged. She knew Seth was right, but in following his plan, she lost everything, including her name.

Seth wanted to comfort her by wrapping his arms around her but did not possess the wherewithal for such a gesture. Instead, he backed away and whispered, "Stay in this room. Don't make any noise. If Wesley wakes, the plan is over before it begins. I'm going to the Rigby Hotel to pick up your clothes. I'll get Wesley's things too. I'll be back soon."

"Won't someone at the hotel be suspicious if you pick up our stuff?"

"I'll tell them Wesley needs his things. Mrs. Rigby will understand."

"Do you really think your plan will work?"

"It's perfect—just like my milking routine."

The distance from the mortuary to the hotel was four blocks. Normally, Seth loved the stroll, but not today. Each step seemed too long and more strident than usual. When he opened the hotel door, he saw Mrs. Rigby scurrying about, dusting the lobby.

"Isn't this whole thing terrible?" she said to Seth. "The death of that sweet girl and the sorrow of her brother...it's just horrible. Poor Jed, driving hotel guests out to the country and now facing this tragedy with his wedding on Saturday. It's too much. I've told him to stay home."

"Yes, it's all so...sad," Seth mumbled. "I've got the woman's body in the mortuary and the brother in my guest room. He's very distraught. He wants his belongings. I was wondering if I could get the—"

"I'll get the key," Mrs. Rigby said. "The brother and sister stayed in room 208."

With his heart pounding, Seth took the key. He tried not to look in a rush as he climbed the rickety staircase. In room 208, he saw clothing and other items strewn across the beds. He scooped them up and stuffed them inside two worn bags that lay on the floor. In a matter of minutes, he was out of the room and down the stairs.

As he handed the key back to Mrs. Rigby, she asked, "Can I do anything else to help? They were guests in my hotel."

"You have been most kind in allowing me to gather their clothing. I must get back to the mortuary."

Mrs. Rigby nodded, and with that, Seth was out the door and heading down Main Street again.

Once inside the mortuary, he tiptoed down the hall to the storage room. He handed Lydia the bags. "I have a wardrobe of men's and women's clothing next to the funeral parlor. I use the clothes for burials. At funerals, townsfolk are pleased when they see the dead wearing something that was once theirs. But it would be best if you wore Wesley's trousers and shirt when you go to the train station. Can't have townsfolk recognizing their clothes or see me walking with a woman alone. That would arouse curiosity. You need to look like a man."

"Wesley's clothes are dirty. He never washes his clothes. They stink. Still, if you think it is for the best, I'll put them on."

"Don't forget his hat," Seth said. "You'll make a handsome man."

He tried to laugh but found he couldn't. "It's nearly six o'clock. Time goes by fast when there's too much to do. I must make the coffin before we head to the train station. Every time someone dies, I say to myself, 'Make an extra coffin. Have one ready for the next time.' Do I do it? No."

Lydia's smile was brittle as she said, "Make sure my coffin is pretty."

"I'll make the prettiest coffin Rooster Creek has ever seen. It will take me about three hours. It's a long time for you to wait, but we have no choice. We cannot leave the mortuary until the sun is down and darkness conceals our movements. You must be hungry. I'll grab some funeral food from the icebox."

Returning with an assortment of leftovers, Seth handed a plate of yesterday's goodies to Lydia.

"You're a kind man," Lydia said.

Seth's eyes moistened with gratitude as he shut the door, leaving it slightly ajar.

Lydia removed her clothing and slipped on her brother's pungent pants and shirt. Seth hurried to his woodshop. From a stack of pine lumber, he picked out enough boards to make a coffin. Making coffins was both a sorrow and a joy to Seth. Death made the coffin necessary, and joy came from constructing coffins of infinite beauty. Today's task was different. This coffin would never hold a dead body. Seth cut the lumber and skillfully nailed it together to create a three-by-six-foot elongated box. The lid was always tricky, for Seth insisted on carving a name. This time, the name was Lydia.

Satisfied with his woodwork, Seth cut satin to cover the interior of the box. Totally engrossed in the task, he was startled to see the shadow of Sheriff Thurston lurking by the open door. He was always intimidated by the sheriff, like everyone else in Rooster Creek, but now he was unnerved.

"You seem a little jumpy, Seth," the sheriff said. "That tragedy out at the bridge has the whole town on edge."

Trying to hide his emotions, Seth slowly replied, "Have a seat,

Sheriff. You may learn a thing or two about making coffins. There's an art to woodworking."

"Can't stay. I just wanted to stop in and take one more look at the body to confirm some details for my report. I knocked on your door, but no one answered. So I figured you were in the woodshop. I don't want to disturb you. I'll come back later to see the body. How are you getting along with that crazy brother?"

"Wesley?" Seth said. "He fell asleep as soon as we got the body inside. Last time I checked, he was snoring. Hope he doesn't miss the funeral."

"I spoke with Bishop Bailey. He thought tomorrow at noon would be a fine time for the funeral. He doesn't need time to prepare; he always says the same thing. Does that time work for you?"

"Tomorrow at noon is fine with me," Seth answered briefly.

"Do you want me to stop in and talk to Pete Jensen about digging the grave?"

"That would be a big help, Sheriff."

"No problem, Seth. Hey, that coffin may be your finest yet. Take care of yourself so you'll be around to make my coffin."

Sheriff Thurston gave Seth a jovial slap on the back and departed.

Seth sat down for a minute to catch his breath. He had not anticipated the sheriff stopping by. He was a little less certain of his plan when he lined the coffin. But not once did he wonder why he was being so meticulous with his work when no one would see the satin.

As he finished the last corner of the lining, Seth looked outside at the moon and figured it was nearly eight o'clock. No longer having a coffin to distract his thoughts, he felt fidgety. To calm his fears, he picked up an old rusty bucket, walked to the garden, and pulled up some carrots. Only his shaking hands revealed he had a secret.

9

ANN GOLDING

At nine o'clock sharp, Seth gently knocked on the supply room door. There was no answer.

"Ann, Ann," he said quietly. Pushing the door more ajar, he could see Lydia sleeping. In a louder voice, he called, "Lydia."

Lydia stretched and opened her eyes. "Is it Frank? Make him go away."

"It's me, Seth. It's time to head to the train."

"I'm so tired."

"Soon you'll be seated on the train. You can rest then. Let's go."

When Lydia stood up, Seth could see she was fully dressed in Wesley's old clothes.

Seth chuckled. "I was right. You do make a pretty man. Don't forget to take the hat."

They walked silently down the hall, out the backdoor, and into the darkness. Their route was easy—a half block to Main Street, six blocks down to the railroad tracks, and a short stretch to the train station. The route was not the issue. The issue was not being seen while staying together.

"An empty ditch runs parallel to Main Street," Seth said as he took Lydia by the hand. "Jump in the ditch if you see anyone. Move quickly but silently. Don't drop my hand. As we get closer to the Rigby Hotel, there may be a light on in the lobby. At the hotel, we'll cut through the alley. Once we pass the business district, it's a straight shot to the railroad tracks. If we get separated, follow the tracks to the train station."

When Lydia squeezed Seth's hand, he stopped his nervous rambling. He squeezed her hand back.

"Hunch down low. Let's go."

The first half block was without incident, except for Seth almost tripping on a sidewalk crack. Main Street posed the bigger challenge. Seth and Lydia avoided walking straight down the street, although darkness would have hidden their movements. They walked close to the buildings. They had no problems passing the bank, drugstore, or post office. But as Seth looked back near Betty's Diner, he whispered, "Stop!"

Lydia froze. They waited for a few seconds.

"I think someone is following us, but I can't see anyone. It's too dark. There's no movement. Stay low just in case. Edge yourself a little closer to the diner. We've got to be sure no one is following."

"It's Frank," Lydia said. "He's found me."

There was no sound in either direction, so Seth inched forward. At the Rigby Hotel, a light was on in the lobby. Seth knew Mrs. Rigby had given Jed the night off, and with Mrs. Rigby there in the day, Seth was sure Fred Rigby had the night duty. He was just as sure that Fred was sleeping on the couch. But there was a chance he was awake and looking out the window.

"Let's go through the alley," Seth said. He crouched down and motioned for Lydia to do the same.

As they made their way through the cluttered alley, they heard a sound like an empty bottle being kicked. Seth sat down, pulling Lydia with him. "There's someone behind us. Stay still."

"I'm frightened," Lydia said softly.

"We'll make it," Seth said, swallowing his own fear.

When they heard no other sound except a dog barking in the distance, Seth prompted Lydia to keep moving.

"Stand up. We must hurry. Do you see the oak tree at the end of the ally? Run to the tree. When you're behind the tree, I'll catch up." Once safely at the tree, Seth saw no other choice but to go up Main Street. "It's dangerous to be on the street," he said. "I think we're being followed, so we need to walk in the ditch. Here—hold my hand and walk fast."

As they made their way through the weeds and tall grass that lined the ditch, Seth said, "We're nearly to the railroad tracks. Can you make it?"

Lydia's reply of "I think so" was unconvincing. But she took a deep breath and moved forward.

With two blocks separating Seth and Lydia from the train station, there was little to fear, except a shadowy figure following behind. They moved swiftly beside the tracks to reach the back wall of the train station.

"Wait here," Seth said. "Crouch down near the bush. I'll go inside and buy a ticket."

"Don't leave me alone in the dark!"

"I'll just be a minute. Scream if anyone approaches."

Frantic, Lydia reached out and grabbed his hand.

Seth pulled away. "You have to stay hidden."

Seth hurried to the front of the station and looked through the window to see who was inside. He was relieved to see only the young stationmaster—a high school friend of Jed and Karl.

"How's that horse of yours?" Seth asked as he entered the station and approached the young man. "I hear rumors your horse can beat Eliminator any day of the week."

"My horse is faster, all right. Have you heard about the accident at the bridge?"

"Got the body at the mortuary. It's too bad about that woman, so young and all."

"I talked to the woman and her brother when they came in last night on the train from Nebraska. I gave them directions to the Rigby Hotel. Have you talked to Jed? Too bad he was driving Rigby's buggy."

"Jed's pretty broken up. Don't want to change the subject, but a nephew of mine has been visiting from Vegas," Seth said. "Unexpectedly, he needs to return home as soon as possible. Family problems or something like that. I'm sure it has nothing to do with staying in the mortuary with corpses decaying in the parlor—always been a troubled kid. He's waiting outside. I'd like to buy a ticket for him to board the ten o'clock train."

"That'll be 15 bucks."

"Here's twenty," Seth said, handing the stationmaster a twenty-dollar bill.

"The train will be here in a few minutes," the stationmaster said as he handed Seth a ticket and five dollars in change. "Good thing you came when you did."

"Thanks. My nephew and I will wait on the platform till the train arrives."

Seth then nonchalantly walked out the front door. When he knew the stationmaster couldn't see him, he hurried around the building to find Lydia.

"I've got the ticket," he said. "In a moment, you'll be safely on the train. Forget about Frank. You'll never see him again. I'll take care of Wesley. You'll be fine."

The train whistle blew.

"That's it. Walk with me to the platform."

Watching from the platform, the train came to a screeching halt. Lydia turned to Seth and said, "Thank you. You're the kindest..."

"All aboard," the conductor yelled.

Seth pulled a fistful of bills from his wallet and handed them to Lydia. At another time, she would have protested, but there was no time for that.

"As Wesley would say, 'I've been born again,'" Lydia said over the hiss and steam of the train. "I promise to keep our secret."

Seth smiled. "Go."

Lydia moved swiftly to the open door of the passenger car. The conductor extended his hand to help who he thought was a young boy climb the two stairs before finding his seat. Lydia looked anxiously out the train window into the darkness, searching for Seth. Like a flickering candle, she saw him wave goodbye.

Seth waved until the train lurched and huffed away. He turned and hurried for home without speaking to the stationmaster again. Along the route, he stopped every now and then to see if he was being followed. There were shadows and sounds, but no person appeared. His mind turned from shadows to the next task at hand. Nothing was more important than getting the coffin ready for the burial.

When he reached his workshop, Seth went inside and carefully laid sacks of oats in the coffin. He put the lid on top. Believing he had a few minutes, he carved a heart under Lydia's name. He then nailed the lid to the coffin with a dozen sturdy nails. *The difficult part of the evening is over*, he told himself and headed to the mortuary.

"Where have you been?" Wesley asked as Seth walked inside. "I've searched the mortuary. You weren't here."

"What are you talking about?" Seth asked.

"I woke up and went to the funeral parlor. You were gone, and so was Lydia. Where have you taken her?"

"Taken Lydia?" Seth paused, his hands starting to shake. "Oh yes! While you were sleeping, the strangest thing happened. The bump on Lydia's head became infected or something. I tried all the remedies and concoctions in the storeroom to remedy the problem, but nothing took down the swelling. The bump grew larger and larger, causing her beautiful face to become grotesque. It was very upsetting. I carried Lydia's body out to the barn and put her in the casket. The casket is nailed tight as a drum. She was so beautiful. I didn't think it right for people to see Lydia so marred. I would have asked your permission, but you were sleeping."

"I have been pleading with the Lord forty days and forty nights for the power to raise Lydia from the dead like Jesus raised the daughter of Jairus. The Lord has granted me that power. Take me to the barn and open the casket so I can call Lydia to arise and come forth. Tonight is her resurrection."

"It's late. It's nearly eleven o'clock. You must be hungry. I have delicious funeral food in the icebox."

At the mention of food, Wesley no longer spoke of his power to raise the dead or of Lydia.

"Do you have chocolate cake?" Wesley asked. "It's my favorite. Mother used to make it with leaven just like the Israelites made their bread."

"Sure do. Chocolate cake is a specialty in Rooster Creek. Can't have a funeral without chocolate cake. It wouldn't be right."

As Wesley followed Seth to the kitchen, there was little relief for the undertaker. Doubt about concealing Lydia's miraculous survival flooded his mind. He had never experienced greater anxiety than what now harbored and laid anchor in his heart. It crept over him like a morning chill as one consequence after another lined up like soldiers ready to aim and fire. *What if Wesley insists on seeing the body? What if Lydia reconsiders and returns? What if I can't live with this lie?*

After Wesley munched on a slice of cake and made quick work of the crumbs, he went down the hall to the guest room to finish his night's sleep without a word about seeing Lydia's body.

For Seth, there was no point in going to bed. Anxiety would not allow him to escape into sleep. He tried to read the Bible, but his reading was superficial. The words barely registered in his mind. He prayed for peace and, for a moment, felt that tomorrow he could tell the truth. Lydia would still have her freedom—or would she? Wesley would surely go to Vegas to find her, and the sheriff would jerk his mortician's license so fast that not even the dead would speak on his behalf. Seth knew in time that his anxiety would fade, but not tonight. To calm himself, he turned his thoughts to Lydia. They had been the only two people on the station platform. No one else boarded the train. She was safe. He envisioned her happy.

THAT WAS NOT EXACTLY the case, at least not at first. Lydia sat in a small compartment with three other passengers. Each one kept to himself or herself, but they often looked up to stare at the young boy.

With nothing else to occupy her thoughts, Lydia's mind ruminated on her short time in Rooster Creek. She found her heart clinging to the small town that had only one rooster. She thought of handsome Jed—the farmer she had kissed and hugged. She thought of Wesley fixing her hair just as her mother had done. She thought of Seth Warenski, who risked his reputation and profession for her happiness. As the train moved farther from Rooster Creek into the dark shadows and red rocks of southern Utah, these gentle memories pushed aside her anxieties, and she slept.

"We're in Las Vegas. The last frontier—the last stop for this train," the conductor shouted as he walked between compartments, waking up passengers. "You need to get off the train. If you are transferring to another train, check with the stationmaster at the depot."

Lowering her voice, Lydia called out to him. "Sir, did you say we're in Las Vegas? What time is it?"

"It's five in the morning, young man," the conductor said, looking down as he passed her seat.

"I'm dizzy," Lydia said in her most masculine voice. "Could you help me stand and get off the train?"

The conductor kindly assisted the young man. "There's a policeman over there," he said. "Should I holler and have the policeman get you a doctor?"

"I'll be all right."

"You look pale."

"You've been most kind," Lydia said.

Walking slowly and unsure of her footing, Lydia made her way from the platform to the train depot where it was warm inside. She walked to the nearest bench and sat down for a moment before asking for directions to a restroom. The young boy walked into the restroom, changed his clothes, and emerged as a beautiful woman. In the new rays of the morning light, no one saw the transformation. Lydia now felt more like herself, but with clarity came panic. She walked back inside the train depot and took a seat on the same bench.

"You look frightened," a woman said to her. "Where are you going next? Are you alone?"

The question caused Lydia to reflect on the fact that she had no idea what came next or how to start a new life as Ann Golding. *Would it have been better to stay in Rooster Creek with Wesley?* Rather than respond to the woman or reason through possible ideas, Lydia resorted to the only answer she knew all too well—tears. The woman came forward, put her arm around Lydia's shoulders, and held her tight.

"There's a boardinghouse down the street. It's not the best but not the worst either. Would you like me to take you there?"

Lydia nodded, tears still flowing down her cheeks. Having a place to stay might not be a bad first step.

The two women walked arm in arm from the train station. At the boardinghouse, the woman went to the dining room, where breakfast was being served, and ordered eggs, toast, and orange juice for Lydia. The woman made arrangements with the landlady for a room. When Lydia finished eating, she was told the woman had paid for her meal and room and was gone. Lydia thought of Wesley and the parable of the Good Samaritan. Although she felt gratitude for the woman, she never liked the parable when Wesley told it. She felt relief knowing that he was not at the boardinghouse to witness the charity and expound on its biblical similarities.

In her small room, Lydia slept. She awakened around noon. Staring for several minutes at the harsh shadows slanted across the ceiling and wondering what was next, she knew nothing could be done until she got out of bed. She got up, went down the hall, showered, washed her hair, and braided it into an elaborate coil. A few minutes later, she walked out onto the streets of Las Vegas. About a block away, she saw a marquee that read, "Ralph's Diner." She walked into the diner and sat down at a small corner table. Without looking at the menu, she ordered turkey on rye and a glass of water.

When the waitress returned with her sandwich, Lydia asked, "How do you like working here?"

"It's a job," came the blunt reply.

"Is the owner here?"

"That's him behind the counter."

Lydia watched as the owner talked with a customer. He seemed friendly enough.

Lydia paid her bill, gathered her courage, and asked the owner if she could speak with him.

"This is as good a time as any," the owner said. "What's up?"

"If you need a waitress, I need a job."

"Have you had any experience as a waitress?"

"I worked at a diner in—" She paused mid-sentence.

He smiled. "Well, if you can't tell me where you're from, can you tell me your name?"

"Lyd—" Again, she paused. "My name is Ann Golding." The unfamiliar name felt awkward in her mouth.

"I understand," he said. "Women come to Vegas to leave their past behind. When can you start?"

"This afternoon."

"See you at two o'clock.

Lydia returned to the boardinghouse and asked to rent a room on a long-term basis. As she signed for the room, she wrote "Ann Golding" and smiled.

10

THE FUNERAL

Seth didn't have to rummage through a closet looking for something to wear. Every funeral was the same—a black coat two sizes too small and black trousers that came above his ankles. Dressed in mourning clothes befitting the funeral of Lydia Birch, Seth went downstairs to wake Wesley, who was sleeping again in the guest room. As Seth opened the door and approached the bed, a shiver of fear crept over him like a prickly porcupine. He put his shaking hand on Wesley's shoulder. "Time to wake up, Wesley," he said nervously. "It's nearly ten thirty in the morning. Lydia's funeral is at noon."

Wesley didn't stir.

"It's time, Wesley. Everyone in town knows about the accident at the bridge. Townsfolk will gather at the cemetery within the hour. If you want to give a eulogy, you'll need time to prepare. Wake up."

Wesley rolled onto his back and pulled the blanket over his head before shouting, "Do you expect me to say something at the funeral of my dear sister in this crooked town? It would be like speaking to heathens in Sodom and Gomorrah."

"I'll make you a bowl of oatmeal," Seth said, ignoring his comment. "You can eat in the wagon. We need to hurry."

"This is a day to mourn the dead and a day to lament that my sister ever met Jed Dawson. It is not a day for feasting."

"Meet me outside in fifteen minutes. I'll need your help carrying Lydia's casket from the woodshop to the wagon. Meet me there."

After pacing back and forth in front of the woodshop for a good twenty minutes, Seth saw Wesley walk out the back door. Without saying a word, he passed by Seth and walked inside the woodshop to find the coffin.

"The finger of God cannot lie," Wesley whispered as he gazed at the casket. "The Lord has etched her name on the coffin and in his heart. Blessed be the name of Lydia."

"Grab the far end of the casket," Seth said.

"Like the Israelites asked to carry the Ark of the Covenant, I now carry blessed Lydia." When the coffin was carefully placed in the wagon bed, Wesley turned to Seth again. "I didn't know Lydia weighed that much. A ton of water must have soaked into her body. That casket weighs at least 150 pounds."

Seth climbed up on the buckboard and instructed Wesley to do the same. As they made their way up to the hilltop cemetery, Seth's hands were shaking uncontrollably. *What if Wesley tells the sheriff that the coffin is too heavy? What if the sheriff insists the coffin be opened?*

Seth would have continued along this train of thinking had Wesley not blurted out, "Where's the Easter Lily?"

"It's autumn, Wesley," Seth said. "Leaves are changing colors. It will be months before Easter."

"Where are the lilies?"

Arriving at the cemetery, Seth pulled the wagon close to the open grave dug that morning by Pete Jensen, who boasted of digging a six-foot hole quicker than any man in the county. Instinctively, Seth walked to the back of the wagon. Wesley followed, singing, "She is risen. Lydia Birch is risen today." Seth and Wesley took the coffin out of the wagon and set it parallel to the open pit. Seth placed a rope under each end of the coffin so he and three other men could lower the pine box into the grave.

"I'll go prepare the eulogy on that bench back there," Wesley said.

"Come back when you see townsfolk gathering."

Wesley nodded and slowly walked to the bench, leaving Seth alone.

Seth retrieved a rake to clean up the area around the gravesite. No one was better than Pete Jensen at digging graves, but in Seth's mind, Pete never finished the job. Engaged in the task, Seth did not notice Sheriff Thurston approach him. He jumped when the sheriff said, "Looks like you are all ready for the service."

"You startled me, Sheriff," Seth said. "You're early. Come to help me rake?

"Just wanted to see how you're coming along," the sheriff said. "Looks like everything's ready. Any chance I could have a look at the body?"

The sheriff moved closer to the coffin, opened a pine nut, and tossed a shell into the open grave.

Unnerved by his comment, Seth stepped backward and landed on a round rock. He lost his balance and almost fell into the burial pit.

"Careful there, Seth. Are you trying to upstage a corpse? More people would come to the funeral if that were the case."

"When you didn't return last night, I wrongly presumed you no longer wanted to see the body," Seth said, knowing his words tumbled out in a nervous ramble. "I've nailed the coffin shut. There's not time to go back to my woodshop to get a hammer. You don't have a hammer in your wagon, do you? It would take me an hour or so to go to the woodshop and come back. Can you greet the mourners for me? We could start the funeral late."

"Don't worry about it."

Trying not to show how relieved he was, Seth asked, "Are you sure?"

"No problem. We all know the cause of death was drowning. Looking at dead bodies is not my favorite thing anyway," the sheriff said as he cracked open another pine nut.

Seth noticed Bishop Bailey and his wife, Gertrude, walking up the cemetery. Bishop Bailey made his way to Seth and Sheriff Thurston. "I'm not too early, am I?" he asked. "Have you got everything set?"

"Seth's got everything ready," Sheriff Thurston said. "The best undertaker in the state."

Bishop Bailey nodded and said, "I couldn't agree more."

Before today, Seth would have soaked in such praise. This autumn afternoon, he looked away from Bishop Bailey and the sheriff and went back to raking.

Karl and his parents were the next to arrive. Mr. and Mrs. Ward insisted on accompanying their son, though they didn't know the young woman who had died.

Bishop Bailey shook hands with Mayor Ward and asked, "After I start the funeral service, will you lead us in prayer?"

Mayor Ward liked praying at funerals though people complained that his prayers were too long, and he enjoyed the sound of his own voice a little too much.

Some arrived as a token of sympathy, having heard about the accident at the bridge. Most came out of curiosity, hoping to see the legendary beauty in the coffin and hear scriptures shouted by her crazed brother.

Exactly at noon, Bishop Bailey, who started every meeting on time, stood at the head of the open grave. He asked the mourners to move closer to him. As people closed ranks in an almost shuffled step, none dared take the designated position of Sheriff Thurston, who always stood at the foot of the grave as the self-appointed presiding officer. Seth, looking appropriately downcast, stood at the sheriff's side and politely declined his offer of a handful of pine nuts. Karl stood between his parents, twisting and turning nervously, looking toward the road, expecting Jed to arrive. He never came.

"Wesley," Seth called over his shoulder, "come forward. As family of the deceased, I have a chair for you next to the bishop."

The mourners waited as the small, bearded man slowly walked over and took his seat.

In his religious voice, Bishop Bailey announced that the funeral of Lydia Birch had begun. With reluctance, Sheriff Thurston removed his light-blue Stetson hat. Mayor Ward prayed for each person present by name, thanked the Lord for the autumn leaves, birds in the trees, and whatever animal might be in the cemetery. Mabel Crosby sang, "I Know that My Redeemer Lives." All silently agreed that she knew the words but not the melody.

When Bishop Bailey began his sermon with, "Dearly beloved, we are gathered today," more than one man rolled his eyes and looked disgusted. But in reverent silence, they listened as the bishop cleared his throat. "We are gathered to honor Lydia Birch. We remember the great sorrow of her brother, Wesley Birch, who sits with bowed head at my side. Our hearts go out to Jed Dawson, who has taken to his bed and is unable to be with us today. I am told that Jed was driving Lydia and Wesley Birch to see our lovely mountain resort when their buggy overturned, and all three were thrown into the raging river below. Jed risked his life to save Wesley Birch, but try as he might, he was unable to save Lydia Birch."

Seth had intentionally positioned himself where he could keep an eye on Wesley. During Mayor Ward's prayer and the hymn by Mrs. Crosby, Wesley looked straight ahead in a blank stare while continuing to pluck his beard. But when Bishop Bailey spouted words of praise for Jed Dawson, Seth saw Wesley's whole body stiffen. The muscles in Wesley's face tightened as he gritted his teeth. He shook his head and closed his eyes tightly. Seth could see his lips silently form the word, "Liar." Nothing was said aloud.

Following the bishop's remarks, Wesley was asked to say a few words. He stood up and said, "Can you all hear me?" In unison, every head nodded. "I will now give my speech. Listen carefully, for I will just say it once." The mourners leaned slightly forward as if straining to hear his every word. When Wesley knew he had the attention of all, he yelled, "An eye for an eye!" and sat down. Few at the funeral understood his words except for the sheriff, the undertaker, and Karl, who stared at Wesley and wondered what evil he had planned for Jed.

After the coffin was carefully lowered into the burial pit, the short funeral service concluded. Townsfolk stayed around too long, some expressing condolences to Wesley. He refused to acknowledge anyone spoke to him. Most talked to each other about the accident. Several cornered the sheriff to make sure their facts were right. As for Seth, he forced himself to go to Wesley and offer words of condolence. "I'm so sorry for your loss." Then, as if reading a well-known script, he said, "I know Lydia's in a better place. You'll see her again."

Wesley did not look up. He knew Seth's condolence was canned. Seth knew it too. He had missed the mark. There wasn't enough emotion in his voice. There were no tears. Realizing he could do better, for a moment Seth forgot that Lydia was not dead, and the coffin was filled with oat bags. With tears in his eyes, he said to Wesley, "I am sorry."

Wesley looked up and thanked him.

"Pete Jensen will be here soon to cover the grave," Seth said. "Let's go to the shade tree."

While the tall undertaker and the short bony man walked arm in arm to the tree, Sheriff Thurston broke away from what was becoming an inquisition about the accident and walked to the tree as well. "I'm deeply sorry for what happened to you, Mr. Birch," the sheriff said in a soft voice. "I hope you'll find comfort in knowing that your sister is in a happier place. Time is a good friend. The pain you feel now will ease to a dull ache. You will find peace." The sheriff's voice then roughened. "But not in Rooster Creek. You need to move along. I'll pay your train ticket to Vegas." The sheriff pulled a fifty-dollar bill from his wallet and handed it to Wesley. "By nightfall, I want you on your way. There's a ten o'clock train leaving Rooster Creek for Vegas. Be on it." The sheriff then turned away from Wesley and walked back to the curious mourners.

Though Seth witnessed money pass from Sheriff Thurston to Wesley and saw Wesley walk out of the cemetery and turn on the road that led to Main Street, he had a sinking feeling the small man had no intention of leaving Rooster Creek. He wanted to follow him and offer him a ride to the train station but couldn't. Fear gripped his soul.

Then, just as suddenly as he had walked away, Wesley turned around and walked back to the cemetery. As he approached, Seth called out in his nervous rambling manner, "Would you like to come home with me? You must be very hungry. I picked up your suitcase at the Rigby Hotel while you were sleeping. You can stay in the mortuary until your train leaves."

When Wesley was standing next to Seth, he said, "I came back to give you a chance to answer a question."

"A question?"

"Do you believe me?"

Seth paused, swallowing hard, and took a deep breath. Like a flashback, he remembered Lydia telling of a kiss and a hug. He wondered if his remembrance was etched on his face. Hoping not, Seth said, "Does it really matter if I believe you? All that matters is that you know the truth, and God knows the truth. It doesn't matter what I believe."

"Do you like drama?" Wesley asked.

Seth didn't answer.

Wesley turned away from Seth and walked away. The sun warmed his back, but he did not notice. His eyes were on the road.

11

ACCUSATIONS AGAINST JED DAWSON

"Mrs. Dawson, is Jed home?" Matilda asked.

"Please call me Mom," Mrs. Dawson said. "No doubt you've heard. Jed won't talk about it. I've pieced together what happened at the bridge. Worse than when the river flooded in 1913."

"Is Jed home?" Matilda repeated.

"Jed walked in the house about ten this morning. He went straight to his room and has not come out. He wouldn't even come out for Sheriff Thurston. The sheriff told me about the accident and of Jed saving a man's life. Before he left, the sheriff said, 'Lock the door.'" Mrs. Dawson's scanned her bare walls, worn furniture, and rag rug before speaking again. "What could anyone want to steal in this house?

Matilda shrugged her shoulders.

"It's been like Grand Central Station around here," Mrs. Dawson said. "The mayor and his wife stopped in. 'Not a finer young man in this town than your son Jed,' he told me. Mrs. Ward had nice things to say about you, too: 'Matilda Robinson is the finest young woman in town. I sure hope Karl can find someone like her.' I don't always see eye to eye with Mrs. Ward, but I couldn't agree with her more. Seth hasn't stopped by yet. He must still be at the cemetery. I'm sure he's gotten word Jed has taken to his bed."

"Is Jed all right?" Matilda asked.

"He won't talk to me. He wouldn't talk to the sheriff, the mayor, or anyone. He doesn't even want a plate of food. Imagine, my son not wanting something to eat. I've never seen him like this."

"Could you tell him I'm here and want to see him?" Matilda asked.

"I'll tell him, but I can't guarantee he'll come out. He's been walled up in his bedroom for hours."

As Mrs. Dawson walked down the hall, Matilda waited impatiently, glancing around the parlor at the abject poverty and assuring herself this would not be her life.

"Jed is coming," Mrs. Dawson said as she returned to the parlor.

When Jed entered the parlor, he didn't embrace Matilda.

"I would have come sooner if I had known," Matilda said. "I was at my sister's in Lehi, trying on my wedding dress. If I had known... Could we talk on the porch?"

Matilda reached for Jed's hand. He pulled away. Separately, they walked outside. Matilda sat in a chair on the porch. Jed preferred to stand.

"Did your sister finish the dress?" he asked.

"I'm not here to talk about a dress," Matilda said as her voice filled with tears. "What happened between you and that woman? The town gossips can speak of little else."

Jed didn't ask how she knew. "Accident," he whispered hoarsely. "I was driving Rigby's buggy." He stopped mid-sentence, shook his head, and looked away as if he were alone. Matilda stood up and wrapped her arms around his waist. He pushed her away.

"What happened?" she asked.

"You already know." Then with voice cracking and eyes closed, Jed said, "I can't marry you tomorrow."

"Let's not postpone our happiness. I had a wonderful time with my sister Kathryn. She made me the perfect wedding dress. It has over thirty buttons and..."

Jed didn't interrupt Matilda as she nervously filled the empty space with details of her dress. But Jed's face couldn't hide what his heart felt: nothing.

Sensing she was speaking into a chilly wind, Matilda dabbed her eyes with a handkerchief and ended her monologue.

"You deserve better," Jed said.

"You are a hero. You saved a man from a watery grave. You can walk down the middle of Main Street with your head held high. It was an accident."

"You still want to marry me?"

"What a question. Of course I do! Tomorrow, I'll be Mrs. Dawson."

For a moment, Jed and Matilda embraced. Then Matilda broke away, talking about all she had to do before the wedding. She kissed Jed on the cheek and hurried to the street, confident all was well, even though when she looked back to wave goodbye, Jed had gone inside. He returned to the comfortable loneliness of his bedroom, the photograph of him and Lydia, and daydreams of what might have been.

WHEN THE CEMETERY emptied of mourners and the last buggies moved like obedient sheep down the hill, Seth's favorite ritual began. The ritual would seem odd to the average Joe, but to an undertaker, it was a must. All undertakers knew they had an obligation to stop in front of each tombstone and introduce the newly departed to the underground inhabitants. This time, it was different for Seth. No introductions were necessary.

Seth gleefully tripped from stone to stone, speaking in whispered tones of beautiful Lydia and an empty tomb. He repeated the words of Bishop Bailey's refrain, "Dearly Beloved, we are gathered..." and imitated Wesley's eulogy, "An eye for an eye." With a smile running deep across his face, he told of Sheriff Thurston irreverently cracking pine nuts between his teeth and throwing shells into the open grave and of the miracle of Lydia's rebirth. His favorite was the line from Charles Dickens, "It is a far, far better thing that I do, than I have ever done."

It was hours before the undertaker returned to his wagon. Only the need to milk Buttercup could crowd out his glee and quicken his pace toward home. Seth pulled up on the reins in front of the mortuary. He went to the back door, picked up the milk bucket, and walked at a fast clip to the barn. In his mind, he rehearsed his perfect routine.

Seth relished the process of milking that night, for he needed to resolve in his mind whether his secret was safe in the cemetery. He hardly noticed when Bert Johnson, a farmer from the edge of town, entered the barn.

"Sorry to interrupt you and your sweetheart Buttercup," Bert teased. "I've got a question. Do you know a feller named Wesley Birch?"

Seth was proud of himself for keeping the bucket upright and not kicking the cow as he glanced up at Bert. Only his hands betrayed his knowledge of Wesley.

"As the crew was picking potatoes this afternoon," Bert said, "I saw through the wire fence a bearded old man staring at us. He didn't look menacing or anything like that, just odd. I went over to the fence and asked if he was a stranger in town.

"He replied that he was just strange looking and laughed. He needed a place to sleep and food as he was just passing through. I told him in exchange for helping us pick up spuds, he could bed down in the barn, and Maggie would fix him dinner. He's odd. Really odd. Quotes scriptures more than Bishop Bailey, and I can't stand that pious zealot. Ever wanted to hear the Parable of the Sower and Ruth and Naomi gleaning the fields at least a dozen times in one afternoon? Me neither. He told me that you could vouch for him. He wants a job until harvest is over. Says he'll be here for a few days."

Seth brushed himself off and stood up. "I know Wesley Birch, although it's too long a story to tell. As far as I know, he'd be a good farmhand."

"If you say so, I'll give him a job. Just hope he can keep the scriptures to himself." Bert chuckled. "It's almost suppertime. Time to be on my way—an apple cobbler awaits."

When Bert Johnson left the barn, Seth let out a long sigh of relief, picked up the half-full milk pail, and headed back to the mortuary. His thoughts flittered between Wesley missing the 10:00 p.m. train and Sheriff Thurston mad as a hornet in springtime. Seth shuddered briefly at the thought of the sheriff chomping on pine nuts while tossing his light-blue Stetson hat to the ground. When Seth reached the mortuary, he was spent. *I'm turning in for the night.* Tucked in his bed, he pushed fears aside in favor of thoughts of Lydia having one more night, if not more, to distance herself from the Vegas train station before Wesley headed her way.

As Seth calmed his thoughts and curled into his covers, it was fortunate he didn't know, in the creeping darkness of evening, that Wesley had slipped out of the Johnson barn and headed to Main Street. When Wesley reached Betty's Diner, he took his place next to the front door. Like a barker at a circus, the rite of passage to the diner was through him. From a wooden crate, he gave a speech to anyone coming or going from the diner: "Jed Dawson was going to marry my sister. He killed her instead."

Wiping her hands on a soiled apron, Betty came rushing out the kitchen door to tell the madman to get off her premises. His response was, "Jed Dawson was going to marry my sister. He killed her instead." Betty had a mind to deck him and leave him sprawling on the sidewalk, but customers were watching. Returning to her demure self, she went back inside and telephoned Sheriff Thurston at his home. "There's a crazy man accosting customers in front of my diner. He's waving his arms and shouting that Jed Dawson killed his sister. I could make him stop, but that would drive customers away. What am I going to do with five pies if he keeps haranguing my customers? You going to buy them?" Then Betty looked out the window. "Never mind. He's gone."

Before the sheriff could reach for his Stetson hat or a handful of pine nuts, his phone rang a second time. "Betty, is he back?" he asked.

"This is Fred Rigby. A crazy man is shouting horrible accusations about Jed Dawson in my hotel doorway. I can't have a lunatic shouting those things about my night clerk. It's not good for business. I can't have hotel guests thinking my night clerk is going to make a move on their fair daughters. Get him out of here."

Normally, if there were disturbances after hours, Sheriff Thurston telephoned Deputy Top and gave him detailed instructions on how to handle the matter. Not this night. The sheriff ran out of the house, hitched up his buggy, and drove so fast to Main Street that even Eliminator would've been left at the starting gate. By the time Sheriff Thurston was pulling up on the reins at Main Street, Wesley had moved on to the saloon. Customers egged him on to tell of Jed Dawson and the beauty at the Rigby Hotel. Only one regular customer was not pleased. Jed's father grabbed Wesley and threw him out on the street.

With a crowd of gawkers looking on, the sheriff jumped from his buggy and cuffed Wesley. He charged him with vagrancy and ordered him to sit in the buggy. The sheriff got in next to him, prodded his horse to be quick, and drove directly to the train station. Before the ten p.m. train could whistle or hiss to a halt, the sheriff ordered Wesley to get out of the buggy and stand on the train platform. With his finger pointed at Wesley, the sheriff said, "Be on that train to Vegas. If you ever show your face in Rooster Creek again, I'll lock you up and throw the key away."

It wasn't until he un-cuffed Wesley, motioned to the stationmaster that he was in charge, and heard a conductor call, "All aboard," that Sheriff Thurston turned his buggy around and headed home. He was tired.

Wesley stood on the train platform in the grasp of the stationmaster just long enough for Sheriff Thurston to turn his buggy around. He then wrestled himself free from the stationmaster and ran through the darkness to the Johnson barn as fast as any bony man could. Yet he was not fast enough to keep up with rumors that spread across Rooster Creek like a January blizzard. News of the accident, the madman on Main Street, and the dark insinuations against Jed Dawson nearly burned telephone wires clear through. Farmers brushed aside the rumors as stemming from a raving lunatic, but not their wives. They knew Matilda could not turn a man's head. She was wonderful, the perfect daughter-in-law, but would handsome Jed Dawson want more? There was talk of his father being unfaithful to his wife, being the town drunk, and knowing comments of "The apple doesn't fall far from the tree." It didn't help that Jed's father staggered down Main Street shouting, "My boy is a Don Juan. Not even the beauties can resist him."

1 2

THE WEDDING

Whatever smears were hurled at Jed the day before, they were tossed aside when wedding guests entered the chapel. After all, when it was all said and done, Jed was still the state basketball champion, had saved a man from drowning, and was born and raised in Rooster Creek. There wasn't a better heritage anywhere. If there had been something between him and anyone else besides Matilda, it was yesterday's headline, not today's.

Jed stood in front of the chapel, facing his accusers, now friends again, and tried to smile. It was not the two hundred guests he wanted to please. Standing next to him was his best man, Karl, who had left him on the road the day before. The two had not spoken since. They stood awkwardly together—Jed wearing the suit his mother ordered from the Montgomery Ward catalog at least two years before, and Karl dressed to the nines as if he already had a law degree. Yet Jed looked the calmer of the two. Perhaps his hours in bed had done him good. Karl was fidgety and kept looking down as if something on the floor was stuck to his shoe.

"Stop shaking," Jed whispered. "They'll think you're marrying Matilda."

"Didn't think you'd go through with this," Karl said.

Jed was silent. There was too much to say.

At 7:00 p.m. sharp, Bishop Bailey asked for silence. In his religious voice, he announced the wedding celebration of Jed Dawson and Matilda Robinson, and that Betty would now play her pump-organ rendition of "Here Comes the Bride." At the blast of the first note, like a Pavlov response, guests arose to welcome the bride into the chapel.

Matilda may not have been the most beautiful girl in town, but she was the star Saturday night. The wedding dress transformed her girlish curves into the flowing lines of a woman. Flower girls gazed up at her with adoring eyes as if she were a queen. On either side of the aisle, women's facial expressions assured Matilda that hers was the prettiest wedding dress they'd ever seen. Men gave approving nods to Jed, assuring him his bride was a beauty, and he was the luckiest man in the room.

After Matilda made her way down the aisle, Jed took her hand.

"Dearly Beloved, we are gathered here in remembrance of our departed—" Bishop Bailey started. Catching himself, he cleared his throat and started over. "We are here tonight to marry Jed Dawson and Matilda Robinson. Two fine young people born and reared in Rooster Creek—not in Lehi, our disadvantaged neighbor to the south. If there is anyone who has reason to doubt whether Jed Dawson and Matilda Robinson of Rooster Creek should be married tonight, speak now or forever hold your tongue."

Sheriff Thurston briskly stepped to the front of the chapel to see if anyone objected. Most guests thought the real reason for his moving to the front was to show that he was sporting a white hat that upstaged the bride. Seeing all were in favor of the marriage, the sheriff popped a pine nut in his teeth and motioned for Bishop Bailey to proceed.

"Thank you, Sheriff," Bishop Bailey said. "Now for the formalities." He took a piece of paper out of his pocket, unfolded it, and began to read. Although it was supposed to be a formal reading, the bishop interjected phrases such as "this fine couple," "the Lord is pleased," and "a Rooster Creek marriage."

Bishop Bailey's reassuring smiles were lost on Jed, who was too nervous to concentrate. The bishop's advice to rely on the Lord for strength to live a happy and productive life fell to the floor as if unsaid. Try as he might to focus on the marriage, Lydia consumed his thoughts. When the bishop asked him, "Do you promise to love and cherish Matilda in sickness and in health till death do you part?" Jed paused. It was a pregnant pause that rippled across the room, up the wall, and out the window.

With guests straining to hear, Bishop Bailey loudly repeated the question and added, "You may still have water in your ears from jumping in the raging river to save a man. If you can hear me, raise your hand."

An almost inaudible "I do" was spoken.

Matilda was weeping with relief when she said, "I do."

"I now pronounce you, Jed Dawson and Matilda Robinson, man and wife. Looking at Jed, the bishop said, "You may kiss your bride."

Not willing to relinquish his role after the impassionate kiss, however, Bishop Bailey offered a few repetitive words about a joyous union before asking Mayor Ward to give the benediction and a blessing on the refreshments that would be served in the dance hall next door.

As Mayor Ward stepped to the front, more than one wedding guest knew they were in for a long siege and nestled back into the benches. Mayor Ward blessed the chrysanthemums and the fall flowers that adorned the tables in the dance hall, naming them one by one. He blessed those who put up the decorations. He blessed the refreshments that they would be delicacies from his constituents in Rooster Creek. He thanked his Grandfather Ward for donating the money to build the dance hall and blessed Jed and Matilda that their posterity would stay in Rooster Creek and their sons would play basketball. When he pronounced "Amen," Betty poked her sleepy husband and said, "He said, 'Amen.'"

Few listened as Bishop Bailey reminded guests to speak softly as they exited the chapel. The guests rushed out of the meetinghouse to the dance hall next door, each wanting to be first in line for refreshments and then, of course, to wish the bride and groom a happy marriage.

Never had there been better refreshments—donuts, cakes, pies, eclairs, and candy. As for gifts, no one was stingy. Presents were piled so high it looked like an Egyptian pyramid of intertwined dish towels, linens, pillowcases, washboards, brooms, dishes, and pans. Jed's pockets bulged with silver coins given to him as tokens of esteem.

When a reception line formed, Jed and Matilda took their place at the front of the hall. Seth Warenski was first in line before Bishop Bailey butted in and said, "You saving my place? I'm always first to wish the bride and groom happiness." Seth took a step back out of respect for the position, not the man. In his mind, the bishop used his position to his advantage. Bishop Bailey thought that he had much to say to the newlyweds, but words drained right out of him when there was an audience of two. Seth quickly moved to the front of the queue.

"When I was tidying up around the mortuary this morning," Seth said to Jed, "I found your hotel badge. Can't figure out how the badge got in the mortuary. It must have fallen out of the dead woman's pocket. You'll need this." When Seth handed the badge off, he noticed Jed's hand was sweaty. Seth laughed. "Got the wedding jitters?"

Before Jed could answer, Sheriff Thurston said, "Hate to interrupt, but I've got pressing law work before I sleep tonight. I want to congratulate the bride and groom and give you what every couple wants, a brown bag filled with pine nuts." He whispered to Jed, "Don't believe a word Seth says about me spitting pine nuts in the open grave of that beauty yesterday. Seth's jealous he didn't think of it."

As Jed shook the sheriff's hand and laughed, a commotion was heard near the back entrance of the hall. Someone was shouting.

From the head of the hall, it sounded like "sister...killed...married." At full volume, there was no mistaking the words: "Jed Dawson wanted to marry my sister. He killed her instead." Wedding guests hastily moved against the walls in shocked silence as Sheriff Thurston ran full speed across the hall. Wesley tried to avoid his direct hit, but he had no chance. Wesley fell headfirst to the floor. Before he had time to regain his footing, the sheriff grabbed his beard, swung him around in a circle, put him in a headlock, and dragged him out of the hall. It was a blur except for Wesley's scream. "Not my beard!"

Bishop Bailey stepped in front of the bride and groom and, in an authoritarian manner, said, "Remain calm. The sheriff has appropriately manhandled, I mean, taken down the madman and taken him out of the hall. Cast from your memory this unfortunate disruption and celebrate the joyous union of Jed and Matilda Dawson. I invite Jed to take his bride away. I understand Fred Rigby has offered them his honeymoon suite—room 208."

Before Bishop Bailey had finished his impromptu speech, every man but one had run out of the hall to see Sheriff Thurston in action. The only man who lingered, the bishop's counselor, was badgered by his wife to go outside. "Get out there and find out what's happening. I don't want to be the last to know."

All agreed Seth was the town hero that night. His actions elevated him in the eyes of the farmers more than any preparations he had made for a burial. Seth didn't stop at the sidelines with the other men. He rushed straight up to the sheriff and asked, "Do you want me to call your deputy?"

"I don't need that knucklehead here. He has night duties at the office. Seth, help me calm Wesley down."

Although Seth was the tallest man in town, he'd never been known for bravery. Yet that night, he jumped in the fray when Wesley broke loose from the sheriff's grasp. Seth took a few punches from Wesley as other men stood back.

"How about that undertaker?" one man hollered.

Sheriff Thurston didn't praise Seth for his actions. He was too focused on Wesley. "I took you to the train depot, gave you money for a ticket, and told you to leave Rooster Creek. I warned you what would happen if you ever returned." Then he turned to the crowd of men inching forward. "This is none of your business," the sheriff said. "Get back inside before I arrest the lot of you or turn Bishop Bailey on you. He can sniff out a hypocrite better than any hound dog in town. Get out of here."

Turning to Wesley, the sheriff continued. "You can't go flying pell-mell into a wedding reception and disrupt the whole thing with accusations against the groom. Good heavens, man, show some respect. What do you have to say for yourself?"

"My sister would never have been in the river facedown if it weren't for the reckless driving of Jed Dawson. If you won't punish him, I will. Moses was right: 'An eye for an eye.'"

"When did you stop going to Sunday school?" Thurston asked. "Don't you know Jesus changed what Moses said? You're supposed to love and forgive. None of this 'eye for an eye' business."

"Why don't you talk to Jed Dawson about respect? Better yet, I'll tell him."

Wesley jumped to his feet and ran toward the hall. Seth stopped him in his tracks with one punch. Men gaping through the dance hall windows cheered. Wesley stood up and bolted to the door. Between the sheriff and Seth, Wesley was again brought to the ground.

"Hold him, Seth, while I cuff him," the sheriff shouted.

Wesley struggled, but with his hands bound together behind his back, there was little recourse but to submit.

"We can't have this man running around loose," the sheriff said. "He's dangerous. Help me get him in the buggy, Seth. Come with me, and we'll take him to the county jail. I'll figure it out in the morning."

"What about the asylum in Provo?" Seth asked. "Wesley clearly has mental problems. Hiram Folger could help him think straight."

"Folger couldn't help an old lady cross the street, but he does owe me a favor."

IT WAS LATE when the sheriff, the undertaker, and Wesley arrived at the home of Hiram Folger on the grounds of the Utah State Insane Asylum in Provo. Sheriff Thurston went up to the door while Seth stayed with Wesley.

Folger answered the door in his pajamas. "It's late, Sheriff," he said. "I've been in bed for hours. What brings you all the way to Provo tonight? It can't be a courtesy call."

"I got a madman in the buggy," Sheriff Thurston said. "He needs to spend the rest of his life in your padded cell. Take him."

Jolted by the inference that the sheriff knew how to handle psychological problems grated on Folger's professionalism. Believing a crash course in psychology could change the sheriff's demand, Folger said, "There was a day a physiatrist could do that for you. He could take your man and put him in a straitjacket or put electrodes on him and even put him on a rack to stretch out his impurities, but those days are gone. There's lots of red tape now. The man needs to be examined by a local doctor and stand before a judge and be found incompetent for me to accept him, and that's just the beginning. Sorry you made the long drive for nothing. Tell the Mrs. hello for me."

"I didn't drive all this way to return to Rooster Creek with a crazy man still in my wagon. Have you forgotten who got you this job?" Thurston asked. "You're not as popular in Salt Lake as you used to be. One word from me to the governor, and you're counseling your grandma. I've got a madman in the buggy. He belongs in the asylum. That's all you need to know."

"I'll take him for one night. I'll make sure he's put in a secured room. In the morning, my team of experts will evaluate him and determine if he needs long-term care or should be sent on his way."

"I don't care what your so-called experts find; I'm giving you an order," Thurston said. "You can follow an order, can't you, or has all the psychological jumbo messed with your thinking? Keep him in the asylum until I give the word. Is that clear?"

Despite his degrees and training, Hiram Folger knew Sheriff Thurston had the upper hand. Like a child submitting to a parent, the psychiatrist accepted Wesley Birch as an inmate in the Utah State Insane Asylum that night.

13

SUNDAY MORNING

Wedding guests waved goodbye to the newlyweds as Jed and Matilda left the dance hall. A few neglected the formality as they were still staring out the windows, hoping to catch one more glimpse of the sheriff, the undertaker, and the crazed man.

Jed and Matilda climbed into Mr. Rigby's polished buggy. If anyone standing close noticed Jed's pale face, they attributed it to wedding nerves, not the fact it was the same buggy that had overturned at the bridge, but now looked as good as new. It was a short trip down Main Street to the Rigby Hotel. Matilda clung tight to Jed's arm. Jed was too busy watching the road to notice.

At the hotel, Mr. Rigby escorted the young couple to the room fashioned into a bridal suite. Jed sent up a silent prayer of thanks when Mr. Rigby led them past room 208.

The next morning, the sun rose over Mount Timpanogos and swept its autumn rays across the valley floor. Oak leaves floated by on the foothills, and halfway up the towering mountain, the rays turned crimson red. Once covered with the green of summer, the fields had yellowed. The sky was an azure blue. The famed rooster crowed promptly at dawn, awaking farmers to their duties. Their wives ignored the sound of the colorful bird, opting to rearrange their pillows, turn over, and drift back to sleep. Other than the periodic barking of a chained dog, not a sound was heard in Rooster Creek. Soon enough, the smell of bacon cooking would beckon loved ones out of bed to Sunday breakfast. Church would begin in an hour. All seemed well and right again in Rooster Creek.

At 9:45 a.m., the bell atop the steeple of the white-framed meetinghouse pealed, signaling the hour for worship approached. Bishop Bailey had arrived an hour earlier, smiling brightly and bearing no sign whatsoever of the previous evening. Just like every Sunday, Bishop Bailey was standing next to the front chapel doors waiting to greet blurry-eyed members of his congregation with a firm handshake and a ready smile.

The first to arrive was Sheriff Thurston. He was always first. He unloaded his wife's wheelchair from the buggy. He then extended his hand to lift her from the buggy to her chair. After he'd wheeled her into the chapel to her customary place at the side of the front row and assured himself that she was comfortable, Sheriff Thurston took a pine nut from his vest pocket, popped it in his mouth, and returned to the chapel doors to stand at Bishop Bailey's side as the second greeter.

Seth, who hadn't arrived back at the mortuary until nearly two in the morning, cringed when Bishop Bailey's booming voice greeted him.

"Looking forward to another of your life-changing lessons."

The undertaker felt uneasy. He had not had time to properly prepare his lesson. He'd been busy. There had been a young woman to get to the train station, a coffin to build, the cemetery ground to prepare for the funeral, and a fake burial to perform, plus the late-night drive to and from Provo with the sheriff and Wesley. Besides, Seth hated the scheduled lesson: "As A Man Sows, so Shall He Reap." The subject was too present, especially with events of the past few days.

"Folger called this morning," Sheriff Thurston said to Seth. "I thought that so-called doctor would never hang up. As it turned out,

Wesley wasn't a good fit with the thousand or so patients who call the asylum home. They tried to put him in a room that held over a hundred men. He bolted. Folger said it took eight men and a security dog to get him in a straitjacket and drag him to a small room in the administration building, so they could keep an eye on him. Sheriff Thurston popped another pine nut in his mouth before adding, "That so-called doctor will think twice before ever letting him leave the asylum. Besides, Folger knows his job is on the line if he crosses me."

Next to climb the chapel stairs were Karl Ward and his parents. Karl had not wanted to attend church that morning, but his mother insisted. He reluctantly shook hands with Bishop Bailey and the sheriff but did not respond vocally to their greetings. He felt deeply uncomfortable in the Lord's house and wished he had insisted on staying home.

Five minutes before the meeting started, Jed and Matilda walked up the steps. Earlier, Jed had begged Matilda to stay at the Rigby Hotel, saying, "Next week would be a better time to begin our religious life together."

Matilda gently reminded him that she had not missed a single Sunday service in three years and did not want to miss today, her first Sunday as Mrs. Dawson. The seemingly small disagreement brought a freezing chill to their earlier marital warmth as they walked up the meetinghouse steps. They were not holding hands.

The newlyweds were greeted by Bishop Bailey, who called them "Brother and Sister Dawson." Matilda blushed at the mention of her new name. Jed looked down and did not meet the bishop's gaze.

Then came the welcome from Sheriff Thurston: "Congratulations on marrying one of Rooster Creek's finest. I can only think of one better." He winked and glanced up to look at his wife sitting next to the front row of the chapel. Gripping Jed's hand and pulling him close, he whispered, "Sorry about the interruption last night. If I'd known Wesley Birch was up to something like that, I would've been on guard at the back door. I took him to the train station and thought he was gone for good. You can rest easy now. Seth and I took him to the asylum."

Once Bishop Bailey made his way to the front of the chapel, all knew the meeting would start soon. The worshippers sat on their respective benches as if they had been preassigned and waited for the announcements.

"Brothers and sisters," Bishop Bailey began, "what a week this has been—the accident at the bridge, the funeral of Lydia Birch, the marriage of Jed and Matilda Dawson, and a madman taken by Sheriff Thurston and Seth Warenski to the asylum in Provo. We welcome the peace of this Sabbath morning. Before Sister Crosby leads us in singing 'Onward Christian Soldiers' with Betty at the organ, and before Fred Rigby offers an invocation, I have just one or two announcements."

Lifting a piece of paper from his pocket, Bishop Bailey read, "We thank the men who righted Rigby's buggy at the bridge and polished it for the bride and groom. On Tuesday morning after breakfast, Betty will clear out the tables and chairs in the diner for the monthly quilting bee. Bert Johnson could use some help picking potatoes as the farmhand he hired is now indisposed." He looked up. "Well, that's all the announcements, except with harvest coming on, hobos are arriving daily on the train. A few have started building a camp near the railroad tracks. The hobos will stay in town a night or two before hopping the next train. May I ask the sisters not to turn away a hobo in need—a plate of food will do much to squelch hunger. But for the grace of God go all of us. Sister Crosby, we're ready."

Sister Crosby, with her ample arms moving to the beat of the organ, motioned for the audience to arise. With gusto, they sang, "Onward Christian Soldiers." Veteran Lewis Crosby, with his hand over his heart, high-stepped around the chapel to the beat of the music until his wife shouted in the middle of verse three, "Lewis, take your seat."

Fred Rigby then stood up, walked to the podium, and offered the invocation: "Dear Lord, we thank thee for the peace of this Sabbath morning. May the unfortunate interruption at Jed's reception be forgotten, and may Seth give a good lesson this time, not like last week. Amen."

Bishop Bailey thanked Sister Crosby, Betty, and Fred and invited the children to walk slowly with their arms folded to the back of the meetinghouse for Sunday classes. A stampede of children rushed from their seats before Bishop Bailey could invite all the farmers and their wives to remain in their seats for Brother Seth Warenski's lesson.

Seth went to the front of the chapel. Usually, he had a kind word, a joke, or an observation, but not today. "Our subject this morning is 'As a Man Sows, So Shall He Reap.' What does this scripture mean to you?"

Old Mrs. Smedley, who jumped at every opportunity to comment, shouted out, "It's the Law of the Harvest. If you do something wrong, you have to pay the price. People might think they can get away with something because nobody knows. The Lord knows, and they'll never be happy until they make things right."

"Why don't we let Karl expound on that subject?" Mayor Ward said. "He's studying law in Vegas."

Karl looked down and, in a quiet voice, said, "I don't recall learning about the Law of the Harvest at law school." He then stood abruptly and walked out the chapel doors.

His father watched him exit before turning to face Seth and the congregation. "I don't want to be too personal, but I think most of you were at the wedding reception last night. That man who burst into the dance hall is going to pay a heavy price. He tried to destroy the reputation of my son's dearest friend. That crazy man was trying to stir up trouble in Rooster Creek. The incident is a good reminder that if any of us have hidden sins, rest assured someday we will reap what we've sown. We'll pay the price. It's God's law."

Karl's exit and Mayor Ward's words were not lost on Jed. He started to stand to leave, but Matilda put her hand on his shoulder, indicating she wanted him to stay, and Jed meekly complied. A lively discussion then ensued with Seth as moderator. But as for himself, Seth had nothing to add—no quips, no stories, not even a joke about the cemetery. When the discussion slowed, Seth announced, "Class is over."

Some thought it strange to end class twenty minutes before quitting time. None could recall such an abrupt ending to a lesson, but it didn't matter. Few wanted a Sunday school lesson filled with admonitions about perfection laced with guilt anyway. Wesley Birch was the topic they wanted to discuss.

Jed and Matilda were not the first to leave the chapel. Well-wishers couldn't resist congratulating them one more time. Jed tugged on Matilda's arm, hoping she would make up an excuse for why they needed to hurry. She ignored his tugging, savoring every congratulatory word. When the newlyweds finally untangled themselves from well-wishers, Jed and Matilda walked to the small cottage they had rented from Mr. Ward. It wasn't much—living room, kitchen, bedroom, and bathroom—but it was home.

They had no sooner walked through the door and hung up their coats when Karl came calling. Karl, always the gallant gentleman when a lady was present, talked of Matilda being a beautiful bride before asking Jed to walk with him along the foothills of town.

"I leave tonight for Vegas," Karl explained. "Need a chance to say goodbye. I don't know when we'll see each other again."

"We said our goodbyes at the reception," Jed said, "when you clung to the wall instead of supporting me."

"I'll be here when you get back," Matilda interjected. "It's a beautiful autumn day for a walk."

That afternoon, the two boyhood friends appeared in no hurry as they made their way to the top of a nearby knoll. The weather had slipped past the warmer days of fall, and they felt the first bite of the coming winter. To anyone watching, Karl and Jed were carefree, recalling the times they had climbed that knoll years before. Once they were beyond the piercing eyes of neighbors, Karl was ready to talk.

"Seth Warenski came to see me after Sunday school. He expressed concern that I had walked out of church. He's a kind man, but his visit was too much love for me to swallow."

"I wanted to follow you, but Matilda had other plans," Jed said. "I guess that's how you know I'm a married man."

"My leaving church early is not why I came to see you. I have news about Wesley Birch. The undertaker told me that after he and Thurston wrestled him to the ground, they put him in a buggy and drove to Provo. Did you know they put Wesley in the insane asylum?"

"The sheriff told me. Bishop Bailey announced it over the pulpit. No secrets in this town, except one."

"The big white asylum sits on a hundred acres or so surrounded by a tall fence. Do you remember the place? It was the fence we used to dare each other to climb over on Halloween. I've heard stories of men in white coats forcing the insane to work in the fields, a cannery, and at a clothing factory. The asylum is a sweat shop for crazies but a real profit maker for those in charge. Seth told me that Sheriff Thurston plans on keeping Wesley locked up in that madhouse forever. Only Thurston can say if Wesley is free to leave the haunted mansion—not medical doctors or administrators. Sheriff Thurston has too much power for a man who can't say two sentences without popping a pine nut in his mouth. Thurston has political cronies in Salt Lake who could kick Superintendent Folger out of Provo with one phone call."

"It's better for Wesley to be locked up with crazy people than hanging around Rooster Creek screaming, 'an eye for an eye,'" Jed said.

"Wesley Birch is not insane," Karl said. "He's an odd duck. Never heard anyone quote so much scripture in my life. He shouldn't have barged in on your wedding reception. That was wrong. But it would not have happened if we had told Thurston the truth. Wesley would have boarded the ten o'clock train after his sister's funeral. You should have been at the funeral. I kept looking for you at the cemetery. Where were you?"

"I'm a married man," Jed said. "I've put the accident behind me. I've put Wesley Birch behind me. You've got to put this behind you too. You're in law school, and I've got a bride."

"Let's tell Sheriff Thurston the truth. Let's clear this up. Matilda will understand."

Jed looked at the ground and shook his head slowly. "I'm not going to tell Thurston everything that happened at the hotel and 'clear it up' like you say. It's none of his business. I'm trying to forget about the accident, but I'll never forget Lydia. She was truly the woman of my dreams. By tonight, you'll be on the ten o'clock train for Vegas. Memories of the accident, Lydia, and Wesley will quickly fade. I've got a bride waiting for me, and there's more than one dancing girl in Sin City anxious to meet you. Forget this! Wesley is crazy. I didn't kill his sister. It was an accident. The bridge was slick. I wish you would understand."

Jed headed back to his honeymoon cottage and Matilda's embrace. This time it was Karl who stood alone. He was the logical one—the one who could always bring reason to any discussion. But not this time.

14

THE WAITRESS

Lydia put the last dish back on the shelf and dropped her soiled apron in the laundry pile late Sunday afternoon. Nightlife in Vegas was starting to move to the streets, and she was headed home.

As she walked the two blocks back to the boardinghouse, Lydia passed by women in low-cut dresses wearing high heels, making their nightly debut. Catcalls from men with wads of money free for the taking promised the beckoning women a night on the town. The excitement of Lady Luck was palpable on every sidewalk and a little too intoxicating for a farm girl from Nebraska who knew better. She had a brother who could call down fire and brimstone and destroy Sin City with just one word sent heavenward. Wanting to appear above the steamy side of Vegas, Lydia watched as the autumn sunrays retreated in the sky. She clung tightly to her Nebraska upbringing as if it might slip from her grasp.

She had much to think about that had nothing to do with the sparkle of streets alive with forbidden pleasure. There was the undertaker holding her hand, pulling her through the alley in Rooster Creek, train passengers staring at her girlish looks seeping through her manly clothes, and the woman who paid for her food and lodging that first night in Vegas. But her overriding thought on that autumn evening was a sense of pride in landing a job at the diner on her first day in town. She had done that on her own. No Wesley to nudge her forward with scriptures sprouting out both sides of his mouth. No Seth holding her hand, assuring her a better life awaited. No woman paying for her to succeed against all odds.

Lydia quickened her pace as she passed by the crass nightlife of Vegas, relieved when she finally arrived at the porch of the two-story boardinghouse. Without stopping in the dining room where a dozen other young women like herself were waiting for dinner, Lydia climbed the stairs, pulled on the light cord, and entered her cell-like room. The room was not chilly, but she was trembling. It wasn't the laughter climbing up from the dining room downstairs that unnerved her or strangers on the crowded sidewalks below; it was the crushing loneliness that crouched in the corner of her room, biding its time until she returned to sit alone as the clock ticked down the empty hours.

Lydia fidgeted with the strands of her hair and accepted the loneliness that weighed on her like a heavy coat. That night, like the night before, Lydia retired to a narrow bed. Unable to sleep, she allowed dark questions to twist and churn into a knot of regrets. Seeking relief, she turned on her side with her knees pulled up to her chest and her face against the wall. No matter what position she chose, despair would not allow happiness to enter the room.

Lydia moved from the bed to the window and tried to lift the bottom panel. Like her life, it was stuck. It had always been stuck. Using both hands, she pulled harder, but the window wouldn't budge. Frustrated, she pounded on the windowsill until her clenched fists could no longer bear the pain. As she pressed her forehead against the window, the reflective glass revealed a ghostlike face surrounded by bedraggled, long hair. With her right hand, Lydia clasped a fistful of hair and held the crumpled mass above her head, extending it as high as she could reach. Her hair held memories of everything and everyone she once held dear, as well as her present anguish.

When she stood up, standing in a position she had often seen Wesley take when he was receiving inspiration from on High, an unsolicited idea flooded her troubled mind. She whispered aloud, "That's the answer."

Lydia ran from the room, taking the flight of stairs two steps at a time until she descended to the floor below. She knocked on the landlady's door and waited impatiently.

When the door slowly opened, Lydia asked, "May I borrow a pair of scissors and a needle and thread?"

The landlady left the door to fetch the needed items. When she found them, she handed the items to Lydia without saying a word and shut her door. Lydia stepped away from the door and ran back up the stairs to her room. She sat on the narrow bed, her right hand opening and closing the scissors with a crisp *whish whish* as though practicing for a great performance. With her left hand, she separated a handful of hair from the rest of the tendrils, and with a sharp irreversible snip, the hair spilled neatly to the floor. Hoping not to make a mess of it, her left hand moved another unsuspecting clump of auburn locks into place as her right hand moved the scissors at a crisp snip. As forefinger and thumb tightened on strands with blades moving sharply, the floor next to Lydia's feet darkened with the hairdo of yesteryear.

No longer would she look like the farmer's daughter lost in Vegas.

Next was her dress. Lydia had learned from her mother how to remake a country dress. Her mother would have been surprised that Lydia could make a country dress the envy of women who walked the streets at closing time. The hemline was taken up, sleeves were shortened, and the wide skirt was made form-like. As for the high collar, it was replaced with a scooped neck. Buttons were neatly sewn down each side of the dress to accentuate her figure.

With a bobbed hairdo and wearing the tight, skimpy dress that neither her mother nor Wesley would approve of, Lydia looked at her reflection in the window and knew life was better. She cleaned up the shorn locks and fabric scraps and tossed them into the fireplace at the far corner of the room. Her hair twisted and turned in the flames to escape its fate, but soon all that remained was a pungent stench and Lydia's knowledge that tomorrow would be a new day in every way.

Sleep came easy that night. In the early hours of morning, Lydia awakened to begin her day. As she walked out into the sun's rays, men strewn across sidewalks were beginning to awaken from their drunken stupor. A chorus of piercing whistles followed her the two blocks to the diner. Lydia would normally have brushed off such attention, but not today. She soaked it in. At 6:45 a.m., she opened the door to the diner.

"What happened to our farm girl?" Ralph asked. "Never seen such a quick change from farm to Vegas. I wondered when Vegas would make its appearance."

Ralph then called the waitresses from the kitchen. "This morning will be busy," he announced. "Five incoming passenger trains will arrive at the station before noon. Ann will welcome customers and serve at the front tables."

"She's only been here a day!" the waitress with seniority exclaimed.

Another called out, "I've been here over two years and never waited on the front tables."

"Ladies, please," Ralph said. "Today is your lucky day. Mine too. I'll be standing at the cash register reaching for money." Looking at Ann, he added, "Lady Luck has just walked into the diner."

At seven o'clock, Lydia opened the diner door. The crowd of men she'd passed on the sidewalk had already lined up. Some might have said they came for Ralph's famous silver-dollar pancakes, but not even Ralph thought so. The waiting line wrapped out the door and past the telegraph office.

Men from all walks of life came into the diner that morning and counted themselves lucky to get a table. None failed to notice Lydia, but she knew how to ignore them and go about her business. It was an innate talent she had learned while working at the diner in Nebraska. No matter how businesslike Lydia sounded, nothing detracted from her stunning beauty as she greeted one and all and led them to a table or a spin-around seat at the counter.

To her question of "What can I get you this morning?" came lustful replies. Lydia laughed coquettishly and reminded customers, "I'm not on the menu."

Most were content to order the silver-dollar pancakes with a branded silver dollar in the middle and an egg over easy with hash browns and bacon. Taking orders, picking up orders, clearing off dirty dishes, and wiping off tables as customers waited to be seated was a demanding juggling act, especially when the cook couldn't put food on the plates in a timely manner. It meant more time to talk with customers, fill coffee cups, and make promises that orders were next in line.

That morning, the customers were like a blur of humanity: faceless and nameless except for one overly dressed and flashy man who smoked a big cigar and played with silver dollars like they were loose change. He joked with Ralph that his diner might make more money this morning than he could make all night at the casino. After staring at Lydia too long, Ralph said, "She's my ticket to fame and fortune. I've hired the prettiest waitress in town."

The flashy man took a seat at a front table. He ordered the customary pancakes. As he waited for his order, he struck up a conversation with Lydia.

"New here?" he asked.

"Came in on the train."

"You like your job?"

"There's nothing like taking orders."

"Can you dance?"

"Not according to any boy back home or my brother, who insisted Christian women never danced."

"I can't teach beauty. But I have someone who can teach you to dance. I own Jack's Casino three blocks down. I'm hiring. No soiled aprons at my place. I pay better than Ralph, and the hours are shorter."

"I need to check on your order."

As Lydia walked back to the kitchen, she thought of Wesley. She had never been good at keeping track of the days, but she figured Wesley had attended her funeral and stayed in Rooster Creek to make sure the undertaker put a proper cross on her grave. She was sure he then went to the train depot and bought a one-way ticket to California. That would be Tuesday—tomorrow. He would avoid getting off the train in Sin City unless he received a revelation to call sinners to repentance. If he got off the train in Vegas, he would walk to the first diner. She was vulnerable. Wesley might walk to a casino to call out sinners, but he'd never step foot in such a den of iniquity. She'd be safer as a dancer in the casino.

Returning to the flashy man holding a wet cigar between his teeth, Lydia placed his order on the table. "What time should I be at the casino?"

"Come at six. I'll have Jane meet you at the entrance. You'll be on stage tonight."

Lydia smiled. Around 11:30 a.m., when it looked like the crowds would ease up, Ralph told his waitresses, "I just got word the train from Utah has finally come hissing into the station. It's really late. They had brake problems up the line in Mesquite. Passengers will be in a huff. Plan on serving breakfast 'til noon."

No one stepped off the train more in a huff than Karl Ward, the young man from Rooster Creek who had come to Vegas to become a lawyer. Karl hadn't slept a wink last night. Wesley crowded every corner of his thoughts. He and Jed had done some crazy things, like putting rotten eggs in the heating pipes at school, and placing a mouse in Mrs. Saunder's sewing room, but they had never injured anyone before. Jed may have already forgotten about Wesley being unjustly incarcerated in the asylum, but not Karl. According to Karl's moral compass, Wesley was on the front burner and taking every inch of center stage. The small, bony, scripture-screaming Wesley could not be blotted out.

Hungry and out of sorts, Karl walked to the familiar diner, hoping they were still serving their breakfast menu. He was surprised to see a line of men waiting to get inside. He debated with himself about whether to wait, but he knew what he wanted for breakfast. Nothing but Ralph's silver-dollar pancakes would satisfy him.

When Karl inched his way to the front door, Lydia greeted him. "Welcome to Ralph's diner. We have one spin-around seat at the counter, or you can wait for a table."

"Are you new here?" Karl asked. "You look familiar. I've come in the diner dozens of times, but I've never seen you here. I'll wait for a table in your section."

"That will be a front table. I'll find you when one becomes available."

It took some time for a table to open, but Karl didn't care. He watched Lydia's every move and was surprised that a waitress could fill Wesley's place in his mind so quickly. Perhaps Jed was right.

Fifteen minutes later, Lydia said to Karl, "The third table is open now. Follow me."

Karl would have followed Lydia anywhere.

"Would you like a menu?" Lydia asked.

"I don't need to see a menu. Does anyone ever order anything besides the famous pancakes?"

"Not if they're smart," Lydia said as she placed a glass of water in front of him.

"Have we met before? When did you start working here?"

"I started working a day ago. Arrived in Vegas on the train and got a job."

"I just got off the train. I'm not looking for a job, though. I'm a law student here in the city."

"You are younger than most of our clientele," Lydia said. "Few come in the diner wearing knickers and white-flannel trousers."

"I came from a farming town in Utah. The town is so small that it takes just one rooster to wake up the whole town."

Lydia stumbled, her hand hitting the glass of water, which fell into Karl's lap.

"Usually, I get a laugh with that line, not a bath."

Lydia hurried to grab a towel. Handing it to Karl, she apologized.

Karl laughed. "You could get fired for being so clumsy."

"It doesn't matter. Today's my last day at the diner."

"Here one day and gone the next. That's a pretty quick turnaround."

"I'm going to be a dancer at Jack's Casino. I start tonight."

"My best friend told me there would be a dancing girl in Vegas anxious to meet me."

"It's not me," Lydia said.

With that, Lydia walked to the front of the diner and got Ralph's attention. "I quit. I'll come in later for my money." As she was walking out the door, Ralph called her name.

"Don't quit. I'll give you a raise."

Lydia ran as fast as she could down the two blocks to the boardinghouse. She didn't feel safe until she had slammed her door shut, climbed into her narrow bed, and pulled the covers over her head.

15

THE "IT GIRL"

Snuggly tucked in her narrow bed, Lydia could think of nothing besides Rooster Creek. Although she traveled hundreds of miles on the train away from Jed, Wesley, and Seth, she was thrust back into Rooster Creek as if she had never left. Lydia cursed God, the restaurant, and the smartly dressed customer from a town that had only one rooster.

This was the roaring twenties, and it certainly roared throughout Vegas. Lydia wanted in. She didn't want to break her parents' musty age-old morals and jump into unadulterated hedonism, but she did want to dance and shimmy to ragtime music. She wanted to go to speakeasies and jazz clubs where patrons danced the night away to the sound of orchestras, big bands, and loud singers. She wanted to be a flapper, a jazz baby, and a star of the silver screen. She wanted to be an "It Girl" like Clara Bow, who made the flaming-red upper lip and steamy dark eyes the signature look of the twenties. Instead, Lydia was trapped in her narrow bed in Rooster Creek.

It took hours to convince herself that she was no longer governed by the stodgy rules of her brother, for she was no longer Lydia Birch. Jack's Casino was but one step in creating her new life. It was a step that would take her away from farmers, religious zealots, chivalrous gentlemen, and modest ladies into an intoxicating, forbidden world. When she convinced herself that the run-in with the customer from Rooster Creek was a fluke, she was ready to leave. She pulled herself up and made plans for the afternoon.

She would stop at Ralph's Diner and get her money. She wished she could go to the telegraph office. There was so much she wanted to say to Seth Warenski, her last link to Rooster Creek. She wanted to tell him of her newfound freedom, cutting her hair, applying makeup, and tossing out dowdy fashions for a shorter, slinkier, more form-fitting dress. She wanted to tell him of the gap between the rich and everyone else who had come into the diner, but there was an oath of silence between her and Seth—the promise that they would never communicate.

Dismissing the telegraph office, Lydia planned to go straight from the diner to the casino and meet Jane, whoever she was. With plans firmly set, her excitement erased the young customer at the diner with his flannel trousers and memories of Rooster Creek. She would soon be on stage. After brushing and tossing her hair and straightening her dress, Lydia ran down the stairs and out of the boardinghouse into the bustling world of Vegas. Catcalls followed her steps to the diner, but her mind was elsewhere. The glittering lights of the stage beckoned.

A stop at the diner proved less than joyous. Ralph made a spectacle of himself begging her to stay and offering everything but the cook. Lydia passed the telegraph office and did notice there were no customers inside. On a whim, she entered.

"Excuse me, sir," she said to the sleeping telegrapher. "Didn't want to wake you but..."

"No problem, young lady," the telegrapher said, rubbing his eyes. "How can I help you?"

"I want to send a telegraph to Rooster Creek, Utah."

"Rooster Creek? Is there such a town in Utah?" After thumbing through pages of his well-worn directory, the telegrapher located what he was looking for. "There is a Rooster Creek. It will cost you twenty-five cents a word."

"Send a telegraph to Seth Warenski, undertaker at Rooster Creek. Write two words—*dancing* and *casino.*"

"That's it? Dancing and casino?"

Lydia nodded and paid the man two bits and walked out. She felt pleased with herself and briskly walked the three blocks to the main drag of Vegas. The glittering signage on Jack's Casino could be seen for a block. The casino doors were flung wide open as if hoping to catch every gullible gambler that strolled down the street. Lydia stepped inside and saw men gambling away their fortunes. Those wearing jackets with wide lapels and comfortable trousers were easy prey for card sharks. They were the ones with the most money and had the greatest talent for losing it fast.

Lydia stepped up to the bar. "Do you know where I can find Jane?" she asked the bartender. "I don't know her last name."

The bartender laughed. "No last name necessary. Every man knows Jane."

Just then, a hardened woman approached.

"You Ann Golding?" she asked, sizing up Lydia quickly. "Jack has always had an eye for beauty. Hope you can do more than attract men. Can you dance the Charleston or Lindy Hop? Have you ever won a dancing marathon?"

Lydia shook her head.

"I didn't think so," Jane said. "Where did Jack find you? At a diner?"

At Lydia's sheepish nod, Jane laughed. "Follow me. You have lots to learn before the show tonight."

Jane walked quickly down a narrow hallway, expecting Lydia to keep up. They entered a dressing room lined with hundreds of outlandish outfits suitable only for a dancer. Jane wasted no time in pulling a dozen dresses off the racks.

"Try these on," she said to Lydia. "You can change behind the curtain in the corner. I'll decide which outfit works for tonight. There is makeup behind the curtain. Layer it. Can't have beauty dimmed by lights."

As Lydia tried on dresses one by one, Jane had much to say—little of it flattering. Jane wanted the right look for the debut—silky, chic, and provocative. Dresses with dropped waistlines, which gave Lydia a straighter profile, were discarded. Outfits with clumsy buttons that hadn't been replaced with hooks and eyes were tossed to the floor. The low-cut, silky red dress, totally unbecoming for a farmer's daughter, caused Jane to exclaim, "Perfect! Bee's knees. Grab silk stockings and a strain of pearls on the dresser and follow me."

Jane led Lydia to the stage where dancers were rehearsing for the night's performance.

"This is Ann Golding," Jane shouted above the trumpet, piano, drums, and tap dancers. "She doesn't know how to dance. Help her hear the beat and sway with the rhythm. Jack wants her in the front tonight."

The dancers gathered around Lydia. Most had been at the casino for just a few weeks. Many had stories of living on a farm, but there was no time for storytelling. They knew what it was like to be the "new kid" and wanted to help. When they saw Lydia's awkward dance moves, none could suppress laughter or ridicule.

"Where are you from, babe?" one asked. "The Ozarks?"

"Didn't your daddy teach you how to dance?" another asked.

"Are you dancing to the words?" another giggled.

There were tips galore, enough to stuff a suggestion box. No matter what they said, Lydia could kick her legs and strut across the stage but could not follow the beat. The turkey trot, which demanded jumping from side to side and kicking feet in a scissor-like manner, proved formidable. Doing the shimmy required more concentration than Lydia had. The Charleston, with knees bent and arms waving in time to a repetitive beat, was fun but not for Lydia.

Jane, who paced back and forth, talking to herself about what she was seeing, yelled out in exasperation. "This is not working. We have less than a half hour before the curtain rises." Turning to Lydia, she said, "It will take more than one afternoon to make a dancer out of you. Tonight, you will carry placards announcing the next dance number."

Lydia was shown where the placards were stored behind the stage. The rehearsal went forward, with Jane acting as director and master sergeant. Each time a new dance number was announced, Lydia dutifully walked across the stage holding the corresponding placard.

The curtain rose exactly at eight o'clock p.m. to a crowded room of men. Jack welcomed everyone with a few inappropriate jokes before saying, "The first dance number is the Charleston. Sit back and enjoy the show."

That was Lydia's cue to walk on stage holding the first placard. From the moment she stepped onto the stage, whistles were deafening. The gyrations of the favorite Charleston proved an aside to the main performance—Lydia. When Lydia walked out with a placard for the second number, men stood up and gave her a standing ovation, and so it went throughout the entire program. The men could care less about the dancers as they shouted, "Bring back the woman with the card."

When the program ended, a few men rushed to the stage, reaching for Lydia. She was afraid. Perhaps this wasn't what she wanted after all. It was too reminiscent of the diner in Nebraska and Frank Cromwell. Lydia fled from the stage to the dressing room. She hurriedly put on her cotton dress, washed her face to get off the makeup, and walked with head down straight out the casino's front doors. She had several blocks to walk in the darkness of evening to reach the boardinghouse.

"Where are my pancakes?" a man yelled as she exited the casino. "It's a long time to make a customer wait."

Lydia looked up and saw the man from Rooster Creek that she met at the diner. The words, "Oh, no!" escaped her lips.

"Hold on," Karl said, reaching out his arm as she tried to skirt around him. "I've come to give you a ride home. Nothing more. Sin

City isn't safe for you after dark. Cops and politicians take bribes and look the other way but never the unbridled man."

Lydia paused and looked up at Karl, knowing the truthfulness of his words.

"Besides, I've had plenty of women turn me down, walk away, say they never wanted to see me again. I get that. But I've never had any woman quit her job because I spoke to her, and there is something about you that is so..."

Karl was interrupted by an intoxicated man who grabbed Lydia's arm. "You're mine tonight, baby."

Karl pushed the drunken man aside with some force. "She's with me. Back off." Turning to Lydia, Karl said, "I've got a Model T Ford outside. I'd like to take you home. You'll be safe, but I do insist on a few rules in my automobile. There will be no spooning, no necking, and no stopping at the Wedding Chapel of Love."

"You have a car?"

"I got it a month ago as a bonus for signing with a law firm in Vegas. Henry Ford makes a car any color you want, as long as it's black."

"I've never ridden in an automobile."

"It's parked up the street around the corner," Karl said.

Lydia looked at the intoxicated man, then back at Karl before saying, "I'd like a ride."

As Karl and Lydia walked to the car, Karl was chatty, and Lydia was guarded.

After they were seated in the car, Karl said, "For starters, what's your name?"

"Ann Golding."

"Well, Ann Golding, what brings you to Vegas?"

"Wanted a change," Lydia shrugged.

"Where did you come from?"

"Far away," Lydia said, keeping her face forward.

"Should I assume you don't want to tell me?" Karl put his hands on the steering wheel.

"That's right," she nodded.

"Well then," Karl said, looking outside the window, "where am I taking you?"

"I am staying in the women's boardinghouse near the train station."

"The star of the show—the 'It Girl'—staying in a boardinghouse?" Karl said, eyebrows raised.

"I wasn't a star," Lydia rolled her eyes. "I carried placards on stage. I'll look for a new job tomorrow."

"Going to quit already?" Karl asked. "What about wanting to be a dancer?"

"I can't dance," Lydia sighed. "They tried to teach me the Lindy and the Charleston. Couldn't do it."

"You can do it. You just need better teachers. You proved your worth to the owner of the casino tonight. You can call your own shots. Want to dance? Just tell them."

Lydia wanted very much to dislike the man seated next to her but found herself thinking of him as kind.

When they arrived at the boardinghouse, Karl stopped the car. He got out, walked around the car, and opened Lydia's door. He asked if he could walk her up to the porch.

Lydia nodded.

On the porch, Karl said, "I look forward to seeing you dance tomorrow night. I'll meet you at the front door and drive you home."

"You'd do that for me?" Lydia asked.

"Count on it," Karl said.

"Same rules—no spooning, no necking, and no stopping at the Wedding Chapel of Love?" Lydia asked.

"Same rules except for stopping at the wedding chapel."

Lydia laughed, and Karl went down the steps to his car.

As he drove to his apartment near the law school, Karl was happy. He hadn't learned why Ann Golding quit her job at the diner or why she looked familiar, but it didn't matter. As for the incident with Jed and Wesley, it seemed forever ago. Nothing was solved. Wesley was still in the asylum, and Jed was cold and distant, but somehow, tonight, it didn't matter at all. Karl had just been with a most beautiful woman, and tomorrow night would be more of the same.

Karl wondered if Jed was really the smart one in their relationship. How could he have known a dancing girl was waiting for him in Vegas? How could he have known that thoughts of Wesley would dim to shadows of forgetfulness? He wondered if Jed was as happy with Matilda as he was with Ann Golding. He assured himself such was the case, recalling Jed leaving him on a knoll in Rooster Creek to return to his honeymoon cottage.

Jed was not happy. Matilda made delicious dinners, kept an immaculate house, and was as attentive as any wife could be. Jed was kind to her but kept to himself. He found reasons enough to be anywhere but home. Chickens in the morning and the Rigby Hotel at night were scheduled daily. In between, Jed needed to check on Eliminator in the barn. Time in the barn stretched to fill hours. Matilda thought the hours away were time needed for Jed to clear his mind of the accident, accusations, and the threats of Wesley Birch.

But no. In a small box under a loose board in the barn, Jed kept the photograph of himself and Lydia. More and more, it looked to him like a wedding photograph. Jed daydreamed of being married to Lydia, and in that daydream, he lost the joy of the present, the joy of being married to Matilda Robinson. Matilda knew something was wrong. Her questions were brushed aside. Loving embraces were rejected. Perhaps Jed could forget about Wesley and even the tragic accident at the bridge, but with the photograph of Lydia Birch ever present in the barn, Lydia was nearer to him than any bride could ever be.

16

NOT CRAZY

K arl returned to Vegas, law school, and a new love interest—Ann Golding. Jed opted for a photograph of Lydia instead of marital bliss and went about his day as if it were a burden. Sheriff Thurston returned to apprehending violators for petty crimes, making it known that his swift actions against criminals made Rooster Creek the safest place to live in Utah. The few who knew of Wesley Birch didn't mention him anymore. The press didn't even have a one-liner reserved for him. Wesley was yesterday's news. He was locked up in the asylum miles away, and that was that.

The exception to such callous disregard was Dr. Hiram Folger, the superintendent of the asylum. He prided himself on his expertise with personality disorders. But when it came to his newest patient, Wesley Birch, curiosity beat out his academic training.

Early Sunday morning, Dr. Folger looked through the observation window in Wesley's door to check on him. Wesley was wide awake, sitting up stiffly on a cot. Dr. Folger went back to his office, telephoned a security guard, and asked him to come quickly. The guard opened the door to Wesley's room and stood next to Dr. Folger as he entered, ready to protect the doctor just in case.

"You look calm," Dr. Folger said. "If I had my assistant take off the straitjacket, would you remain calm?"

Wesley nodded.

With the straitjacket off, Wesley stood and stretched for the sky before bending low to touch his toes, repeating the movement a second and third time.

"I'll speak with him alone," Dr. Folger said to the guard. "Wait in the hall."

When the guard exited, Folger sat on the edge of the cot. "I'm Dr. Hiram Folger, superintendent of the Utah Asylum for the Insane. I've known Sheriff Walter Thurston for longer than I've been superintendent of the asylum. He has brought dozens of patients to me. Each one has been a special case, some certifiably insane and others with nowhere else to go. The first time Sheriff Thurston brought a patient in the middle of the night was last night. He didn't explain what the urgency was or why you were a good fit for the asylum. Can you explain to me what caused the sheriff to be in such a hurry to get you here? I won't interrupt. I'm not the law. I'm just trying to figure out why the sheriff insisted that you be in the asylum."

As Dr. Folger took out a small pad of paper and a pen from his pocket, Wesley looked him over from head to toe. Balding, stooped shoulders, potbelly, and blotchy skin—not a man to be envied for his physical appearance. Wesley could not tell, however, if he was seeing a friend or foe, a Jonathan or a Jezebel. Either way, he had an audience of one to listen to the story that played over and over in his mind like a broken record.

"The story of my being in the insane asylum begins with the death of my parents in Nebraska and ends with the straitjacket lying in the corner. It is a story of tragic proportions that few believe." Wesley cleared his throat and stood before his audience as he recounted the tale.

Dr. Folger's notes on what he heard were brief: "Frank Cromwell was going to harm Lydia...a train from Nebraska to Rooster Creek...

the night clerk at the Rigby Hotel...Jed Dawson and Lydia Birch planned to marry...a wedding photograph...Lydia facedown in the river...Jed Dawson married another...disruption at wedding reception." Dr. Folger was surprised he had written so much due to the difficulty of grasping the storyline when the sentences were punctuated with so many scriptural outbursts. No matter which way Dr. Folger interpreted his notes or Wesley's nonverbal actions, it was clear to him that the bony man with the long beard had been wronged.

"Thank you," Dr. Folger said. "You have unraveled for me why Sheriff Thurston would wake me up in the middle of the night and be so ornery. He told you to leave Rooster Creek and catch the train. You faked him out, stayed in town, and disrupted a wedding reception. You embarrassed him. Sheriff Thurston prides himself on being the Wyatt Earp of Rooster Creek, if not the entire state of Utah, and you blemished his perfect record. You made it look like he hadn't done his job."

Dr. Folger paused, thinking through the story he'd just heard.

"One puzzle solved, now for the next," Dr. Folger said. "I have questions for you, Wesley Birch." Hoping to catch him in a lie, he asked questions that gave Wesley ample room to retell his story in a slightly different way. But no matter how he tweaked the questions, Wesley's answers were always the same.

After a pause of large proportions, Dr. Folger said, "I believe you."

"You believe me?" Wesley asked.

"Yes, I believe you told the truth."

"Hallelujah!" Wesley called out. "Praise the Lord."

"Before you praise the Lord anymore this morning, let me walk through your agenda today. First is breakfast in the cafeteria across the way. At ten o'clock, be back in your room so a staff member can ask you questions like, 'What year is it? Who is the president of the United States? Can you count backward from fifty to forty?' If he asks, 'Do you have feelings of hopelessness?' assure him you're working through such feelings. At eleven a.m., you will be evaluated in the room down the hall by a team of trained specialists."

"Will a scientific stamp of approval by the specialists assure you I'm crazy? Then will that be followed by electric shocks, hot baths, cold baths, and special diets of protein or lack thereof? Or will it simply be a straitjacket that confines me to solitude like the Apostle Paul in Rome?"

"What the outcome will be, I cannot say," Dr. Folger said. "But I hope you have a taste for cafeteria food. It's never been my favorite."

As Wesley walked toward the cafeteria, he couldn't help but notice the grandeur of the asylum buildings and the manicured grounds. But unlike most beautiful places, no one really wanted to live there—especially him. The cafeteria wasn't exactly empty when he entered. Most patients had already risen from the long lines of dormitory beds, eaten breakfast, and made their way to jobs in the fields, the cannery, and the clothing factory. Only a few stragglers remained in the cafeteria, hoping to eat one more breakfast roll to tide them over until lunch.

When Wesley entered, heads turned to watch him. He was new, small, and vulnerable, like many of them, but with his long beard, he looked formidable.

Then one man called out, "No one eats in my house unless I say so!"

Wesley fired back immediately. "You will be blessed for allowing a stranger to dine with you this day." With that, Wesley picked up a bowl of oatmeal and sat next to the man.

The man was pleased. As for the oatmeal, it was one step below mediocre.

At ten o'clock, Wesley answered questions. At eleven o'clock, he appeared in front of the evaluation committee, four men wearing white coats sitting around a large table. His opening remarks were, "The inquisition begins. Judge and jury are before me. Are you Pilate, Herod, King Agrippa, or Judas? No matter the outcome, I shall triumph over all my enemies."

Dr. Folger invited Wesley to sit and confine his remarks to answering questions. Dr. Folger then introduced Wesley to the committee, explaining the incident at the wedding and the late-night drop-off by Sheriff Thurston. He spoke of Wesley's attempt to run away and of his night in a straitjacket.

The questions were probing. Wesley's answers were spot-on: no delusions of grandeur, no imagining himself as a wild beast or a domestic animal. No attempts at suicide, no hospitalizations in the past, and no run-ins with the law, except for Sheriff Thurston. Each answer was couched in scripture, of course. After all, Wesley had an audience, and it was the Lord's day—the day when scriptures unfold to his servants in technicolor. As the evaluation wrapped up, Wesley reminded his judge and jury of the scriptural admonition, "As you judge, you will be judged," before leaving a blessing upon his audience of good health and righteous living.

When Wesley was escorted from the room, the evaluation team had much to say.

"Where he errs is in his fixation on revenge and justice. He could be a threat if he's released from the asylum, but judging by his size, he's like a puffer fish, puffed up but not much of a bite."

"His obsessive behavior is extreme. Did any of you count the number of times he said, 'Jed Dawson' or 'An eye for an eye?'"

"Can you imagine what he'd say about my stopping at Rosie's Saloon for a drink after work?"

"He's a one-note man. He's forgotten how to play the keyboard. He's bright but too focused on one topic—Jed Dawson."

Dr. Folger halted the circling discussion when he was ready for lunch. "We may have months and years to talk about Wesley Birch. The only decision that needs to be made before lunch is this—is Wesley Birch crazy?"

A small piece of paper and a pencil was handed to each member of the evaluation committee. They were told, "'Yes,' means he's crazy, 'No,' means he's not crazy." After each man had written his evaluation, papers were folded and handed to Dr. Folger. The superintendent unfolded the papers one by one and read them aloud. The consensus of the evaluation team in the official report read, "September 26, 1923: Wesley Birch is not crazy."

After lunch, Dr. Folger explained to Wesley the findings of the committee. "Although you have personality disorders that need to be addressed, the evaluation committee found you *not* crazy."

Wesley fell to his knees, hugged Dr. Folger's feet, and praised God.

"Stand up, man," Dr. Folger said. "Let me get on with it. You will not be put in a straitjacket or asked to bed in the long dormitory with the insane. We will create a small bedroom for you in this building. You are free to roam the asylum grounds, but you are not free to leave until I straighten things out with Sheriff Thurston. In the meantime, you will need to help out somewhere on the grounds. Because of your experience as a cook in Nebraska, I'm suggesting that you help in the cafeteria kitchen."

"Not free to leave the asylum?" Wesley asked.

"Not yet," Dr. Folger said. "I'll visit with Sheriff Thurston soon. Oh! One more thing. Seth Warenski, the undertaker at Rooster Creek, telephoned me. He wants to know what type of memorial you'd like on your sister's grave. A stand-up tombstone with her name and the words 'In Loving Memory,' or a ground-level marker with her name and the words 'Gone but Not Forgotten'?"

"I want a cross," Wesley said. "A cross like Jesus had. I want it tall and stately with this inscription running lengthwise down the cross: "An eye for an eye."

"I'll telephone the undertaker, and you can tell him."

"Operator, get me Seth Warenski in Rooster Creek."

"Seth, it's Dr. Hiram Folger here. I've got Wesley Birch with me. He wants to speak with you about the tombstone for Lydia."

Dr. Folger handed Wesley the phone.

"Seth, another time I'd like to discuss with you your part in bringing me to the asylum," Wesley said.

Seth was silent as fear made his hands shake.

"I want a cross put on Lydia's grave," Wesley continued. "I want it tall and stately like the cross Jesus had. I want you to carve Lydia's name on the cross. Under her name, carve a heart, like the finger of God did on her coffin. And there's more."

"I'll be right back. Someone's banging on my door," Seth said. "Don't hang up."

Seth opened the door just as Sheriff Thurston popped a pine nut in his mouth.

"It's about time," the sheriff said.

"Just a moment, Sheriff, let me hang up the phone. Have a seat."

Picking up the telephone, Seth said, "I can make the cross and the inscription, but the size of the cross is a problem. It's really windy up at the cemetery. If the cross is too big, it will fall over. I think a four-foot cross could stand the wind. It would be the tallest monument up there."

"Make it beautiful like my sister," Wesley said and hung up the phone.

"Sorry about that, Sheriff," Seth said, returning to the parlor.

"There's a stranger in town who calls himself Frank Cromwell."

Seth quickly put his hands behind his back so the sheriff could not see that the mere mention of that man's name caused his hands to shake violently.

"He came in on the train. He's been stopping in every town since Nebraska looking for Wesley and Lydia Birch. He claims Lydia Birch was his runaway bride. He spent the day on Main Street asking everyone about the brother and sister and got an earful. Frank knows about the accident at the bridge, the death of Lydia, and rumors about Jed Dawson. He left Main Street and walked out to the cemetery. He read the inscriptions on all the tombstones and couldn't find a grave marker for Lydia. He thinks you've tricked him, and you're hiding his wife-to-be somewhere in the mortuary."

"Frank Cromwell sounds crazier than Wesley Birch," Seth said, looking for a chair to sit on. "Sheriff, what are you doing about it?"

"I visited with Jed on the porch. He's scared. Just when he

thought himself safe in Rooster Creek with Wesley in Provo, here comes a jilted lover. This is a mess. I told Jed not to go to the Rigby Hotel tonight or stay in his cottage. He's spending the night in the barn with his horse. Matilda has gone home to her parents' place for the night. I'm going to arrest Frank Cromwell and hold him in jail. He's a menace and a threat to Jed and you. I think you're safe in the mortuary, but maybe not. You may want to spend the night with Buttercup or, better yet, climb in one of your coffins."

"And I thought this was going to be a peaceful week," Seth said, leaning back in his chair and willing his hands to be still. "Let me think. Sure wish it was milking time. I do my best thinking with Buttercup. But here goes—I could make Lydia's monument this afternoon. By tomorrow, the ground covering her casket should be stable. What if you brought that Cromwell fellow to the cemetery? He could help me put up the memorial to Lydia. That would solve the problem. What time shall we meet?"

"The earlier, the better. I want that man out of Rooster Creek on the morning train heading to Nebraska. Put a shovel in your wagon in case we need to dig up the body."

17

A STATELY CROSS

Seth worked feverishly on the monument that would cast a long shadow over other tombstones in the cemetery. He cut a wooden plank exactly four feet in height and another half the size. On the smaller plank, he carved LYDIA and a perfect heart. Satisfied with his work, Seth nailed the crossbeam to the taller plank and stood the cross up in the corner of his shop. The cross looked dramatically different from the tombstones he had made before, but artistically, it was his best work.

As Seth stood back, admiring his creation, instead of thinking of Christ, Gethsemane, or Calvary, he thought of Frank Cromwell with a shovel in hand, marring the cross, digging up Lydia's grave, opening the coffin, and finding a tomb full of oats. Such thoughts were almost his undoing. Seth shut the door to his woodshop and walked out into the night air. At the mortuary, he drank a glass of milk and got ready for bed. Fear would keep him from sleeping but not from tossing and turning and strewing covers across the planked floor of his bedroom.

But then came a reprieve—a knock at the front door. Seth was used to being awakened at all hours of the night as the dead don't die according to his 9 to 5 schedule. He stepped into his slippers and headed downstairs, hoping the bereaved would ignore his pajamas and the fear chiseled on his face. He was surprised to see Hank Jacobs from the telegraph office.

In a solemn manner, Seth welcomed the telegrapher and invited him to come inside. Seth noticed that Hank didn't look like a man in grief—a man who'd come to tell of his lost love. Hank appeared almost giddy.

"Seth, my news could have waited 'til morning, but I couldn't. Sorry about interrupting your night's sleep. I wanted to see the look on your face when you read the telegram that just came across the wire. Don't get one like this every day."

"Let's sit in the parlor," Seth said. "There's better light in there."

Hank eagerly handed Seth the telegraph. Seth read aloud the words *casino* and *dancing*. His solemn funeral-like face failed him.

"I've told Harriet hundreds of times," Hank said. "The mortician —her beloved Sunday school teacher—has a secret life. For years, Harriet has assured me that I'm wrong. For the life of me, I couldn't figure out where you stashed the women. A handsome man like you sleeping alone in the mortuary didn't make sense. I surmised women were hiding in your embalming rooms, waiting until you pulled the drapes. Now I have primary evidence—a telegram to you from Vegas, the Sin City capital of the world. Now I get it. No wonder one of our lovely women in Rooster Creek has never been able to put her hooks in you. How could a farmer's daughter compete with the leg-kicking sirens of the night? I'd like to read this telegram to Harriet. Would it be all right with you?"

"There's been a big mistake," Seth purposefully chuckled. "I'm sure the telegram was meant for someone else. If not, it's a good joke on me." He paused to look down, and then laughed out loud. "Oh man, that is pretty funny! Can't wait to tell the women in the embalming room about this one. Sure, you can tell Harriet about the telegram, but remember to laugh."

When Hank left, Seth whispered aloud, "Lydia made it to Vegas and has a job dancing in a casino." He was still smiling as he climbed the stairs, rearranged his bed covers, and got back in bed as if sleep might not evade him after all.

There was no need for a lone rooster to wake up Seth Warenski the next morning. He ate a little breakfast before going to his shop, carrying out the cross, and putting it gently in the wagon bed. He then went to the barn and selected his dullest shovel, hoping to prolong the agony of digging up the grave. With the cross and shovel in the back of his wagon, Seth drove the distance to the cemetery. He arrived before Sheriff Thurston and Frank Cromwell, just as the dead retreated back into their coffins. He spoke to them as a group and explained that today would be his last day in the cemetery. The reason was that an empty tomb that brought peace in Jesus's day would not bring peace today.

Like a religious martyr, Seth carried the cross to the gravesite and waited. When no one came the first hour, he stopped clinging to the cross and started digging a deep hole, one deep enough to keep a four-foot cross from falling over. He placed the cross in the hole and said a silent prayer. "Jesus, put in a good word for me, a sinner, who faked a funeral and a burial."

It was not until Seth was sprucing up around the disturbed ground that he saw Sheriff Thurston. He was wearing his cowboy hat and striding alone up the cemetery hill.

"Morning, Sheriff. Where's that Frank fellow?" Seth called out.

"It's a story," the sheriff said, pulling pine nuts out of his pocket and hurrying faster up the hill. "I picked up Frank Cromwell last night. He's a bruiser of a man and could clobber most men, but not me. I shoved him into a jail cell. He was mad as a hornet in springtime. His yelling and banging on the jail bars were louder than crackling lightning in a thunderstorm. Frank cursed me, Lydia, Wesley, and every soul and blade of grass between Rooster Creek and Nebraska. Before he'd calmed down and gotten his second wind to name all the people in Missouri, I had the telephone operator connect me to the main sheriff's office in Nebraska. As it turned out, Frank Cromwell is a wanted man. From Nebraska to Wyoming, officers of the law have tried to capture him but failed. I single-handedly captured a hardened criminal—a man wanted for destroying property, threatening public officials, and the murder of a transient hobo. The sheriff's office in Salt Lake City is sending officers to transport the hardened criminal back to Nebraska to stand trial."

"Didn't expect to hear that," Seth said.

"Wish you could have seen me wrestle that mammoth brute into the jail cell. It was a sight to behold—him punching at the wind and me using great force."

"Bet you weren't popping pine nuts then," Seth said.

"Let me help you get that cross standing straight. Can't have a crooked cross at the cemetery. The bereaved would think twice before asking you to bury their loved ones. By the way, there's no need to dig up the dead body today. I don't have time. I'm heading back to the office. A photographer and a reporter are coming with the lawmen from Salt Lake. I'm going to be featured in the *Deseret News*, *The Salt Lake Tribune*, and in newspapers as far away as Nebraska."

Seth could hardly contain his relief. He didn't hug Sheriff Thurston's feet like Wesley had done to Dr. Folger, but he felt like it. Relief ran in a steady stream from his tall head to his big toe.

He wanted to tell Lydia that Frank Cromwell had been apprehended and was on his way back to Nebraska, but he assured himself that telling Wesley would suffice. Seth was more anxious to tell Wesley, however, of the stately cross that towered over tombstones in the cemetery. Rather than turn his wagon toward the mortuary on that beautiful autumn day, an exuberant Seth Warenski went to see the man wrongly committed to the Provo asylum. He had more reasons than one to see Wesley, but his greatest was to ease his own conscience.

It took nearly two hours to drive his old wagon to the asylum—hours in which Seth did some mighty thinking. Next to milking Buttercup, some of his best ideas came that day on the buckboard. First was Sunday school. There was too much talk about right and wrong in Sunday school, and Seth didn't feel like much of an authority on that subject anymore. With Hank's wife sure to tell all who would listen about Seth's telegram of casinos and call girls, it was time to step down as the teacher.

Then there was the issue of Lydia's grave being disturbed. A new road that cut through a corner of the cemetery was being proposed next week at the town council meeting. Under the proposal, a few graves would be moved—one being the grave of Lydia Birch. Seth concluded that he needed to lobby the town council and Mayor Ward against the proposition.

Then there was his seventeen-year-old nephew, who wanted to assist him in the mortuary and at the cemetery. Seth loved his nephew like a son, but what if he grew curious about the grave under the cross and dug up the coffin? It was a crazy idea, but Seth could not shake it. His nephew would have to find other employment.

Seth next thought of Wesley. It was an injustice to the small, bearded man to be confined in the asylum. It needed to be resolved, if only for his own conscience. Seth comforted himself by saying aloud, "Until then, it is a far better thing than I have ever done before."

A melancholy mood descended on him as Seth neared the asylum. He parked his wagon inside the formidable walls and walked the familiar path to the administration building. There he was warmly greeted by Hester Hempstead, secretary to Superintendent Hiram Folger. Seth was well acquainted with Hester. Years before, she'd been one of his near brushes with matrimony.

"I'm sure you've come to see the superintendent," Hester said as Seth walked in, "since you haven't come to see me for over a year. Well, you had your chance."

Seth looked down. "I've come to see Dr. Folger."

"He's in a meeting," Hester said. "He shouldn't be too long."

"I'll wait in the foyer."

Hester nodded as Seth took a seat and reached for a crumpled magazine to help him bide the time. As he waited, Seth thought of the cross and of Wesley being pleased when he saw it. But that was a crazy notion. Wesley would never get out. He would never see the magnificent cross; Sheriff Thurston would see to that.

It was a half hour before Hiram Folger walked into the foyer and greeted Seth with exuberance.

"Seth! Good to see you. I expect you'll be a regular here the way you talk to the dead. No bodies to pick up today, and you drove all this way. Did you come for Wesley?"

Seth nodded.

"My team of experts pronounced him not crazy, even after he called each one to repentance and shouted, 'judge not that ye be not judged' and 'an eye for an eye.' Can you help me figure out how to get him out of here with Sheriff Thurston's blessing?"

"If you've got a few minutes, Hiram," Seth said, "I'd actually like to talk to you about Wesley Birch before I visit him."

"Come on in," Hiram replied, gesturing toward his office. As the two men settled into the small but tidy office, Hiram said, "Have a seat. I'll pull my chair around so we can talk. I don't like a desk between me and my guests, whether they be visitors or patients. What's on your mind?"

Seth sat back in the chair and interlocked his fingers behind his head. He took a deep breath and asked, though he already knew the answer, "Has it been two or three days since Wesley entered the asylum?"

"Let's see. You and Sheriff Thurston brought him to me late Saturday night. It's been three days."

"I imagine Wesley feels like it's been years trapped behind the tall walls outside."

"That long?" Hiram asked in a musing tone.

"Wesley shouldn't be in here," Seth said.

"Wesley was so full of hate Saturday night that it was running out his ears," Hiram said. "The man was dangerous. He escaped after you dropped him off. It took our best men, me included, and a security dog to capture him, put him in a straitjacket, and drag him to this building."

"It's time to release Wesley from the asylum," Seth said. He hadn't intended to be so bold. His words shocked even him.

Hiram sat back in his swivel chair and hooked his thumbs under his suspenders before saying, "Wesley Birch is as normal as you and me, except for his extraordinary ability to call down the powers of heaven. Why, he'd make a good teacher of religion at that college next door. Wanting revenge against Jed Dawson is a little extreme, but which of us in a moment of passion hasn't wanted to get even with someone who wronged us? Wesley would never hurt anyone—not even Jed Dawson."

Seth shuffled his feet under the chair.

"Like one of our experts said, 'He's like a puffer fish.' He blows up to look big, but he is just a little man. As to his work ethic, after a day in the kitchen cafeteria, he practically runs the place. He has that kitchen humming. Food still isn't good, but it's better. His quirks, which are more than a few, could be cured in an outpatient facility. The only good thing I see coming out of Thurston forcing me to take Wesley is that Wesley likes it here." Hiram chuckled before saying, "He's become popular, a leader of sorts. My patients say it's something to do with his beard. If there was an election in a few months, he'd be elected to take my job. What are you doing Wednesday night?"

"No plans," Seth said as he adjusted himself in the seat.

"Drive that hearse of yours straight back here," Hiram said. "Wesley is putting on a one-man show in the theatre. It will be his version of schizophrenia—Dr. Jekyll and Mr. Hyde. Wesley will be playing both characters."

"Wesley has a flair for show business?"

"Try to come if you can."

Seth politely nodded.

"There's another matter, Hiram. Yesterday on the telephone Wesley told me to put a cross on his sister's grave. The cross now towers over the tombstones in the Rooster Creek Cemetery. It's my best work. I'd like to show it to Wesley. What if I took him back to Rooster Creek today? What do you think?"

Hiram rubbed his chin as he contemplated Seth's proposal. "Seth, you of all people know that I have strict orders from Sheriff Thurston to keep Wesley Birch in the asylum. There would be severe consequences if I released him without the sheriff's approval. Thurston has the politicians in Salt Lake wrapped around his little finger."

Seth would normally have let his proposal drop, but today, he pressed on. "I could take Wesley to the cemetery tonight, teach him some cooking techniques in the mortuary, and have him back to the asylum in time to fix you a sumptuous breakfast."

Hiram didn't move. A corpse could not have looked stiffer. Seth sensed the psychiatrist was at least considering his idea. After a long pause, Hiram muttered, "What you're asking is risky business." He then looked around the room and out the window before adding, "I'd like to give Wesley that chance, but Thurston would have my job, my license, and my reputation. He'd destroy me and do it with pleasure. I can't risk it."

Seth stood up and said, "Wesley could ride with me on the buckboard until we reached Pleasant Grove. I'd have him climb in the back of the wagon and lie flat like the dead. I'll cover him with the canvas I use to cover bodies. No one in Rooster Creek will see us. No one's at the cemetery at night. After Wesley sees the cross and pays his respects to his sister, he can sleep in the mortuary, and I'll keep an eye on him. Remember, it was me who pulled him to the ground at the wedding reception and wrestled him into Thurston's wagon. Before daylight, I'll bring him back to the asylum. I'll be here for his Wednesday night performance too. I wouldn't miss his version of Dr. Jekyll and Mr. Hyde, especially after watching Thurston play both roles for years."

Seth watched the superintendent weigh the pros and cons and get up from his chair and pace back and forth. It was a weighty choice

—the good of a patient versus the good of a psychiatrist. Being a kindly man, Hiram erred on the side of Wesley.

"A wrong can never be a right," Hiram said. "The man has the right to see his sister's grave. My fears of Sheriff Thurston and his political clout in Salt Lake should not hold any weight with the healing of a victim. Wesley told the truth about the accident at the bridge and has been deeply wronged. Seeing that cross would help him push the unfortunate series of events to the background. In so doing, he could embrace letting go of the burden that plagues him." Seeming to make up his mind, Hiram then asked, "Have you ever read *A Tale of Two Cities* by Charles Dickens? Probably not. In that classic, there is a scene where a friend poses as the main character, who was sentenced to death. As the friend awaits execution, he says something like, It is a far better thing than I have ever done before. By allowing you to take Wesley to see the cross, I can say the same thing.

Seth extended his hand, and Hiram took it. Seth hurried out of the office to speak with Hester as Hiram closed the door.

"Hester, I need to see Wesley Birch. Can you get a security guard to find him? I'll wait for him by the front door."

It took about twenty minutes before Seth saw Wesley walking across the manicured lawn.

After a hasty greeting, Seth said, "I've got really good news!"

Wesley scowled and said, "You're gonna throw me to the ground and wrestle me into the sheriff's wagon again?"

"Hiram Folger gave me permission to take you to Rooster Creek and show you the cross on Lydia's grave. How soon can you be ready to leave? You won't need to take much; it'll just be one night. I promised Dr. Folger to have you back in the asylum to fix his breakfast tomorrow morning."

"I'm ready now," Wesley said as his eyes grew to the size of chicken eggs. "I just need to get a few things."

Seth rested his hand lightly on Wesley's shoulder as a friendly gesture, but the small, bearded man shrugged away from his touch.

"Stay here. I'll be right back."

Just then, Superintendent Folger appeared in the doorway. "Listen to Seth Warenski," he said to Wesley. "Do what he says. I hope you are pleased with the cross. I'll see you both tomorrow morning."

Wesley offered no sign of having heard the superintendent. He ran right past him to his room, grabbed his bag, and walked at a fast clip straight to the asylum gates.

Seth turned to Hiram apologetically. "I'll catch up with him. He'll be back before breakfast. You have my word."

18

WESLEY HAD HIS OWN PLAN

Seth walked at a fast clip to catch up to Wesley and lead the way to the wagon. Wesley followed closely behind like a shadow, stretching his strides to match those of the lanky undertaker. Once they reached the wagon, Seth gestured for Wesley to jump up on the buckboard as if he were chauffeuring a celebrity. Catching the spirit of the occasion, Wesley bowed before climbing aboard.

"It's the same wagon that carried Lydia's corpse," Wesley said in an uncharacteristic childlike voice. "Your old horse could hardly pull the chariot with her body in the back. Today should be easier. No corpse to slow us down and angels flying overhead, beckoning us to Rooster Creek."

With a flick of his wrist and the familiar touch of the whip, Seth got the old mare's attention. Getting Wesley's attention was not as easy. He was reciting Daniel's escape from the lion's den and comparing it to his escape from the asylum.

To be heard above the scriptural reference guide at his side and the whirling wind, Seth raised his voice. "With this old mare pulling us, we'll be in Rooster Creek in no time." He then tugged on the reins, and, at a slow, meandering pace, the mare pulled the odd twosome out of the parking lot, past the no-nonsense security guards, and through the asylum gates.

It was then that Wesley's face lost its earlier look of childhood wonder. With the loud cracking of thunder overhead, his bitter murmur was too soft for Seth to hear. "Never thought I'd be on this side of the gate again."

Seth was pleased. *One night away from insanity isn't much for Wesley, but it's a start.*

When an automobile passed them, Wesley said, "The rich have it made but not in heaven. The eye of the needle will put a stop to that. It will be easier for a camel to get through that needle than a man in his automobile."

"The horse and buggy will soon be sidelined by the automobile everywhere except Rooster Creek," Seth said. "We pride ourselves in being dead last to adopt modern ways. If it was good enough for Grandpa, it's good enough for us."

Wesley ignored Seth's words.

Seth saw that Wesley was drinking in the scenery like a thirsty man crossing an arid desert. He changed the topic in hopes of striking up a conversation. "This road takes us past some of the greatest vistas known to man. Mount Timpanogos and pine trees reaching for the sky are at their best in autumn. Why, even the quaking aspens bend to show their appreciation."

Wesley did not comment, even though Seth had set the stage for an oration on Mt. Sinai. It was not until a freight train roared past on tracks running parallel to the road that Wesley stood up and shouted, "More coal cars than boxcars."

"Sit down. Can't have you falling out of the wagon. You've got a lofty cross to see."

Wesley reluctantly sat down but turned his head back and forth so as not to miss a single boxcar. "Look there," he said, pointing at the flatcar. "It's a hobo. Can you see him? He's on the flatcar."

Seth squinted to make out the figure. "I see him."

"I've heard tell that a thousand hobos are crisscrossing the nation on trains. They don't pay a red cent. Look at him—free—totally free."

Like a radio broadcaster on national news, Seth replied rather matter-of-factly, "Our nation's headed toward an awful depression. Some are calling it 'The Great Depression,' but I don't know about that. It doesn't seem any different in Rooster Creek. But there are hobos everywhere—men hard on luck. Rooster Creek has five or six in town right now. They're mostly good-natured fellows. They come around to back doors, asking for handouts. Townsfolks give them food. I do my part. The hobos ask for clothes. I have closets full of clothes, hats, and shoes worn by the dearly departed. Think I should open up an as-is dress shop in the barn?"

Wesley was tired of Seth's constant chatter. When the train roared out of sight, he adjusted himself back into the buckboard. "My father rode railroad cars on a freight train like those hobos. He wasn't looking for a handout at a lady's back door or clothes worn by the deceased. He rode trains to get a preaching job—to call sinners to repentance." Pounding his fist into his hand, Wesley yelled, "A train killed him!"

Seth looked at Wesley. "Your father must have been quite a preacher."

"He passed himself off as a Baptist preacher. Most sinners thought my father wasn't a good preacher because of his thick German accent. He couldn't quote scripture and verse. But sinners plunked down a few coins anyway, making jumping off trains worth his while. I had the makings of a real preacher. I read the entire Bible twice before I was ten years old."

Wesley pulled a stained red handkerchief from his pocket and wiped his nose. Seth sat silently compassionate as only a trained undertaker could.

Suddenly Wesley lifted his hands above his head. "Thank you, Seth, the undertaker, the keeper of the dead, and the snatcher of a soul from endless torment! Because of you—a humble servant on an errand—I'm on my way to Rooster Creek to fulfill destiny: 'An eye for an eye.'"

His burst of happiness had caused Seth to smile, but the part about destiny and "an eye for an eye" made the smile slip off his face. Creeping fear rushed into Seth's mind where peaceful silence stood restrained. The twosome passed through Orem and Lindon lost in thought—both making plans. As dusk settled over the countryside, Seth shouted his plan in Wesley's direction.

"As soon as we get to the mortuary, we'll get something to eat and then head straight to the cemetery. You'll be pleased with the magnificent cross on Lydia's grave. It's my best work."

"Each day in that nuthouse was an eternity," Wesley said. He paused and clenched his fists before hollering, "We never should have stepped off the train in Rooster Creek. Lydia could have been uncoiling her hair right now and reaching for her mother's brush. Who is Pilate? Who is Herod Agrippa compared to the night clerk who killed my sister and married another?"

Seth nervously returned to the subject of religion. "You would've made a good preacher, Wesley. I'll bet you end up smack in the middle of heaven when your time comes."

"I'm not set on going to heaven, but I sure don't want eternal fire and brimstone," Wesley said as he gritted his teeth. "That's what I've had in the asylum. I've had enough of that on earth. As for Jed Dawson, no mansion of glory awaits him. He'll burn in eternal flames. The Holy Bible holds out little hope for a liar."

A knot formed in the pit of Seth's stomach as Wesley cursed Jed to eternal depths and beyond. Seth turned to see if hatred spewed out of Wesley's mouth like a firehose unleashed. There was no blazing fire, but Wesley's head jerked from side to side as his frenzied mind left no room for rational composure. Seth's hands trembled like Mount Vesuvius on the verge of a volcanic eruption.

"What about his horse?" Wesley asked.

"Old man Johnson tried to convince Jed to sell him Eliminator. Fat chance of that. Jed put Eliminator in Mayor Ward's old barn to keep Johnson from taking him. The barn on Jackson Street—that's the one."

"An eye for an eye," Wesley shouted.

In spite of escalating alarm, Seth didn't turn the wagon around and head back to the asylum. Security guards would have opened the gates, and Dr. Folger would have breathed more than one sigh of relief. Seth rationalized that he had thrown Wesley to the ground once and, if need be, he could do it again. His desire to have Wesley see Lydia's cross outweighed his darkest fears. At the "Welcome to Pleasant Grove" sign, Seth pulled on the reins and tapped his mare to move to the side of the road.

"Why are you stopping?" Wesley asked.

"You've got to climb in the back so you won't be seen. Can't chance Rooster Creek folks seeing you outside the asylum. Lie flat, and I'll pull the canvas over you. Anyone seeing me with the canvas pulled up knows there's a corpse in the back. No one wants to take a peek at the dead until I fix them up. You'll have to be under the canvas until we reach the mortuary."

"Is it the canvas that covered Lydia?"

"One and the same. It smells bad, but with the whirling wind and scattered rain, you'll be all right."

Seth jumped down from the buckboard and beckoned Wesley to follow. After hesitating for a moment, Wesley climbed down from his seat and walked to the back of the wagon.

"Tell me again why you want me to hide like Adam and Eve among the trees? You have permission from Dr. Folger to take me to the towering cross of Jesus."

"It isn't Folger I'm worried about. If anyone sees you and reports to Sheriff Thurston that you're out of the asylum, there'll be a mountain of trouble. You and Folger will swing from the gallows, and I'll be stuck in a jail cell. The sheriff told Folger not to let you out of the asylum without his permission."

"Sheriff Thurston is nothing more than a pompous imbecile,"

Wesley shouted, waving his arms. "He couldn't recognize a lie if it bit him on the nose."

Seth ignored the outburst. "Wesley, get in the back now. There's no time to waste. In a few miles, we'll be in Rooster Creek, and you'll be eating a sandwich at the mortuary."

Becoming uncharacteristically docile, Wesley climbed into the wagon bed and lay down. Too relieved that Wesley was cooperating to consider his sudden change in behavior strange, Seth covered the small, bony man with the bloodstained canvas. With nary a peep coming from the back, Seth pulled on the reins and passed through Pleasant Grove. A few people shouted, "Another body from the asylum?"

Seth nodded gravely.

Seth was relieved to reach Main Street in Rooster Creek. He saw a few men walking from Betty's Diner. He shouted to them as if everything was normal, but life was anything but normal.

"Picked up another corpse from the asylum?" they asked.

Again, Seth nodded.

Seth drove his mare and wagon behind the mortuary just like he always did when carrying the dead. He pulled on the reins, and, after straining from side to side to scan the horizon to make sure no one was lurking nearby, he stepped to the back of the wagon. He could tell Wesley was stirring under the canvas.

"Don't say a word," Seth said as he lifted the canvas. Wesley stretched before leaping from the wagon like a freed wild animal. The two men then ran to the back door of the mortuary.

With his long strides, Seth easily took the lead and whispered over his shoulder, "Keep up." Once inside with the door safely shut, Seth spoke again. "The guest bedroom is down the hall. You remember the room. There's a Bible on the nightstand. I'll make you a sandwich. While you eat, I'll milk Buttercup. When I'm done, it will be dark enough to head to the cemetery. You can ride on the buckboard. No more hiding under that bloodstained canvas for you; darkness is a better cover."

Seth left Wesley in the hallway and went to the kitchen. He opened the icebox and pulled out a piece of ham to put between two thick slices of bread, and poured the last of the milk into a tall glass before hurrying to the guest room with supper on a small tray. As he hustled down the hall, he couldn't cast out fearful thoughts that crept into his mind like blood coursing through veins: *Is Wesley gone? Did he run away while I fixed his supper?*

In a frantic burst, Seth pushed the guest room door open.

Wesley was seated comfortably on the bed, reading passages from the Bible.

"Do you know the difference between altars of stone and a stone altar?" he asked.

Relief spread across Seth like a warm blanket after a cold trip to the outhouse.

"Sorry for bursting in like that—an old habit. Here's a sandwich and a glass of milk. I'll be in the barn if you need me."

It was dusk when Seth left the barn with a full bucket of milk and opened the back door to the mortuary.

"Wesley, I'm back," he called as he put the milk in the icebox. There was no answer.

Fear tapped Seth on the shoulder and hissed, "He's gone." Seth tried to squelch it, but when he opened the guest room door and found the room empty, his hissing fear roared into a panic. He stared at each corner of the room, pulled back the bed covering, and looked underneath the bed. Wesley was not there. Seth raced from the guest room down the hall shouting, "Wesley! Wesley! Where are you?" He opened and closed every door in the mortuary. He searched every nook and cranny not once but twice.

Then like a bolt of lightning, Seth thought, *Wesley's in the outhouse. That's the answer. He's from Nebraska. No newfangled gadgets for him.*

Still slightly frantic, Seth ran out the back door to the outhouse. He knew shouting might arouse curious neighbors, but he couldn't help himself. "Wesley! Wesley! Are you in the outhouse? Not a good time to play hide-and-seek."

Ignoring all privacy, Seth flung the outhouse door wide open. No one was there. He went inside anyway and looked at every corner of the small space. He ran to the back fence and looked across the field toward the barn before opening the gate. He ran to the barn and his workshop, shouting Wesley's name with every step. He ran back to the mortuary and into the funeral parlor, passing a mirror that reflected a ghostlike image. With a jolt, Seth stopped and stared. It was him. Blood had drained from his face, leaving his skin as white as milk. No...as white as a decaying corpse.

In a daze, Seth rushed out the front door. No matter which way he looked, he could not see anyone in the encroaching darkness. He ran to the back fence and tried to see through the blackness again, but even the shadowy buildings had retreated from view.

Seth needed to do his best thinking. There was no time to run to the barn and milk Buttercup again. He sat down on the front porch and pressed his hands against his head, hoping the pressure would push the right thought forward. As his mind convulsed and played through a dozen scenarios, there was only one truth that surfaced: *Wesley Birch is out there in the darkest of nights intent on harming Jed Dawson.*

Seth knelt to pray. Words didn't come. He ran to the barn, hooked his old mare to the wagon, and headed to the road, looking everywhere but not knowing where to look.

19

IN SEARCH OF WESLEY

Wesley had no intention of staying with Seth when they reached Rooster Creek, but he was surprised the opportunity to escape presented itself so soon. Few things could distract Seth when he was milking Buttercup. He didn't see Wesley fill a flour sack with food from the icebox or take scissors from the kitchen cabinet, cosmetics from the storage room, and men's clothes and a wig from the burial closet. Seth did not see Wesley cross the field, gleaning wheat as he went, whispering that he was akin to Ruth harvesting the fields of Boaz, nor did Seth see Wesley take a leaping jump into an empty ditch and crawl on hands and knees for a hundred yards with a gleeful grin, like a child who had stolen candy and gotten away with it.

Wesley headed straight to Bert Johnson's farm, this time with no intention of picking up spuds. He tiptoed past the farmhouse to the little shelter on the back of the barn where he had bunked for a night. He found the nearly invisible opening between the shelter and the barn he had staked out earlier. The space was large enough for him to move about on his hands and knees but not large enough for the average-sized man to crawl inside. *When Seth realizes I'm gone and searches the Johnson farm, he will never find me. Not even old man Johnson would think to look in here. I am like Jonah inside the belly of the great fish, waiting to come forth at the Lord's bidding.*

Wesley assured himself that running away from Seth was justified and nothing akin to betraying the Good Samaritan. After all, it was Seth who threw him down to the ground and took him to the asylum. Only the sound of a wagon pulling in the side yard could put a plug in Wesley's musings. He listened carefully to hear Seth's loud thump as he jumped to the ground from the buckboard. Through a small knothole, Wesley caught a glimpse of Seth running frantically from one outbuilding to another. He heard him call out a dozen times or more, "Wesley, I know you're here. Come out." After several minutes, Wesley watched as the more subdued undertaker climbed on the buckboard and rode away again.

Seth drove his horse and wagon down Conder Lane to Alpine Road before turning on Mill Lane toward the cemetery. With each spin of the wheels, Seth craned his head, as if on cue, looking for Wesley, but there was no Wesley or anyone else to be seen at that ungodly hour. Nevertheless, Seth continued to look. As he rode along the familiar road to the cemetery, his mind raced with fearful thoughts, none worse than what revenge Wesley was planning for Jed Dawson.

At the top of the cemetery, Seth stopped to get a better view of the burial ground. The silence at the top was as deafening as the darkness hiding details of the tombs. Yet Seth felt a degree of comfort, for he was among the dead. *He'll come. Wesley will see Lydia's cross.*

As night encroached on his thoughts, Seth took the role of a tyrannical schoolteacher chastising an errant boy. He scolded himself for coercing Dr. Folger into letting him take Wesley out of the asylum and for leaving Wesley alone in the mortuary. He couldn't believe how stupid he had been for telling Wesley that Jed kept his horse in the mayor's old barn. When his thoughts settled on telling Sheriff Thurston that Wesley was a missing person, Seth envisioned the pine-nut-popping sheriff lording over him and insisting that he dig his own grave next to the cross.

Feeling beaten at his very core, Seth thought it timely to walk to the stately cross and beg for mercy. At Lydia's grave on the hill, Seth watched as the moon came over the mountain and slowly arched across the night sky. Growing impatient with waiting, he mused about heading to town and asking at the saloon if any of the drunks had seen Wesley. After all, the saloon was the only business still open and drunks would embrace an undertaker who was known to have a secret life filled with casinos and dancing girls.

Perhaps returning to Bert Johnson's farm was the better choice. He hadn't checked every nook and cranny. Ideas of where else to search fluttered into his mind and departed as quickly as butterflies on an elusive chase.

Seth needed to think, but without Buttercup, his thoughts had nowhere to land. With the night air growing increasingly chilly, Seth went back to the wagon, grabbed the canvas, and carried it up to the cross. He spread the bloodstained tarp on the ground and laid down, looking at the stars for a clue in the heavens as to his next move. He fought to stay awake, but with the canvas pulled warmly across his body, he lost the watchful battle to sleep.

When he jolted awake sometime later, he reasoned, *I couldn't have slept long.* Yet as he pushed the canvas away and stretched his sore muscles, he saw a light in the eastern sky. He turned to see how Lydia's cross looked in the first light of day. He was pleased until he noticed something dangling from the cross: a glistening necklace, the very one he had given Wesley in the mortuary. For the first time on that frantic night, tears filled Seth's eyes. He had not been wrong about Wesley coming to the cemetery, but he was in the wrong for not staying awake.

Seth did not know he wouldn't have recognized Wesley anyway —his looks had changed dramatically. On a bale of rotting straw, he had taken from the flour sack his treasures—scissors, a curly black wig, cosmetics, and men's clothing at least four sizes larger than himself—before kneeling down and crying, "Dear God, thou knowest my vow until now. It is over. Amen." He then picked up the scissors and cut his hair close to the scalp. Next was the beard. He put on the black wig and dismantled the hay bale, stuffing the oversized clothes with straw so he looked like a heavyset man. He then applied makeup to his face, giving himself the look of a weathered sun worshipper.

Wesley walked to the water trough to see his reflection in the still water. Although the night sky blurred the image, the shadowy figure revealed a personage with no resemblance to the bony man who ran away from the undertaker. Pleased with his transformation, Wesley picked up the flour sack and moved quickly to the road. He went first to Mayor Ward's barn on Jackson Street, where he etched "an eye for an eye" with a jagged rock on the barn door. Then Wesley stood back a foot or two to admire his work. *The marquee is ready. The play starring Dr. Jekyll and Mr. Hyde has begun. Will Jed be on time for the opening act? He won't want to miss it.*

Wesley went to the cemetery next. He almost tripped over the sleeping mortician lying near the cross like a sinner begging mercy for past wrongs. Feeling the part of a Christian coming to the cross, Wesley pulled the canvas up over Seth's shoulders to keep him warm before taking the necklace from his neck and hanging it on the cross. He whispered a few words of praise about beautiful Lydia before assuring her that Jed Dawson had no place to hide.

With daybreak peeking through the darkness, Wesley left the sleeping mortician and the cross and headed down the cemetery hill to make his debut on Main Street. Along the way, he saw a pastor picking flowers in the front yard of his parish.

Wesley called to him. "Good sir, may the grace of God go with you this day. May you not be snared by a Sadducee or Philistine on this beautiful autumn morn."

As he walked through the business district of Rooster Creek, sleepy townsfolk smiled at him and greeted him warmly. None suspected that the pudgy hobo was the man who had burst into Jed and Matilda Dawson's wedding reception.

Wesley was more cheerful than one might expect. He took on the persona of a jolly fat man down on his luck. When he passed the pool hall, he hesitated to enter until recalling that Jesus dined with a tax collector and was none the worse. Four men playing pool greeted him with big friendly grins, seeing him as easy prey for the next game. Wesley asked about a hobo camp in town. They told him to keep walking south for a quarter of a mile.

"You can't miss it," one man said. "It was set up a few days ago."

"The Lord couldn't have directed me any better," Wesley said and walked out of the pool hall, whistling "Amazing Grace."

Seth, for his part, saw no alternative to facing Sheriff Thurston. He picked up the tarp and threw it in the back of the wagon. Once seated on the buckboard with reins in hand, he determined to do one more search for Wesley. He headed to town and drove up and down Main Street twice. He saw the pastor standing near his parish, a few townsfolk up and about, and a heavyset hobo walking toward the railroad tracks—nothing more. He circled every block south of Main Street and every block to the north. He went back to Johnson's farm and stopped at the mortuary just in case Wesley had returned. It was then he turned his horse and wagon around and, with a deep breath, headed to Sheriff Thurston's home.

Seth pulled up on the reins in front of the white picket fence that encircled the sheriff's yard. On this day, the picket fence looked like a row of fearless sentinels waiting to attack. Seth unlatched the front gate and walked slowly to the big porch. He didn't know what time it was—but he knew he would awaken the sheriff. Seth hesitated a long while before knocking on the front door. His first knock was too gentle to be heard. When no one answered, Seth pounded his open hand on the door.

He heard Thurston's big footsteps and then his booming voice. "This had better be good. Hold your horses. I'm coming." He opened the door. "Is that you, Seth? You look like you've been up all night. What are you doing here at this hour of the morning?"

All Seth could say was, "He's back."

"Who's back?" the sheriff asked.

"Wesley Birch! Hiram Folger let me take Wesley out of the asylum to see his sister's cross. He ran away from me."

Seth then paused before mumbling, "I don't know where he is."

"Hold on, Seth. Hiram Folger knows better than to let Wesley Birch leave the asylum to go on a field trip to see a cemetery. If what you're telling me is true, Folger is in big trouble." Sheriff Thurston's face grew stern. "Are you saying Wesley Birch is back in Rooster Creek?"

"I looked for him all night. I went to Bert Johnson's farm, the cemetery, up and down every street in town. He's nowhere to be found." Seth put his hands in his pockets and stepped back.

"Wesley Birch is dangerous. When we hauled him out of town, he was threatening Jed Dawson's life. Where is he?"

"I'm sorry, Sheriff, but I don't know where else to look. I didn't want to bother you, but I didn't know where else to turn. I need your help," Seth pleaded.

"You'd better find him, Seth," the sheriff said, shrugging his shoulders, his lips forming a thin line. "You brought him here. You get him out of Rooster Creek. You and that so-called 'Dr.' Folger are in big trouble."

"I know that. I'll accept all the blame. You can send me to prison or wherever you want, but we've got to find Wesley before he hurts Jed. You captured Frank Cromwell single-handedly. Your picture was splashed all over the *Deseret Evening News*. Why, townsfolk have talked of little else since the news broke. If anyone can find Wesley, you can."

Seth's words had the desired effect. Sheriff Thurston's demeanor changed from disgust to highly pleased.

"I can find him, and I will," Thurston said. "Wait on the porch while I get dressed. Nobody's going to harm Jed while I'm the law in

Rooster Creek. If Jed got hurt, it wouldn't just be Folger's reputation or yours that would drop faster than a mallard on opening day of duck season; it would be mine. We can't have that, can we?"

With a wink and a chuckle, the now-pleased sheriff left Seth sitting on the porch as he dressed, choosing a white Stetson to place smartly on his head. When the sheriff returned to the porch, he found Seth pacing back and forth.

He cracked open a pine nut before asking, "Anything else I should know?"

"I've never known anyone more filled with hatred than Wesley," Seth said. "Wesley hates Jed."

"Go back to the mortuary and get some sleep," Thurston said. "You look positively beat. I can handle things from here. Wesley isn't hard to spot—skinny man, long beard, calling down the powers of heaven to send brimstone and fire to destroy Rooster Creek. If I were a gambling man Seth, and I understand you are that type." Thurston chuckled, "Casinos and dancing girls. I had surmised as much. Saw you on the night of Lydia's funeral taking a young boy to the train station. I followed you—alleys, really, Seth? Hardly becoming for a mortician. The stationmaster said the ticket was for a nephew to Vegas. My foot! It was your dancing girl." He stopped to chuckle at Seth once again. "Place your bet on me finding Wesley Birch within the hour. I'll come by the mortuary to collect. Don't squander the money on one of the beauties in the embalming room."

2 0

THE HOBO

Betty had already started cooking scrambled eggs, toast, and pancakes, knowing she could set her watch on Deputy Top and his morning orders. He now sat on a spin-around seat at the counter. Top had been appointed a deputy by Sheriff Thurston, not because he was capable, strong, or could wrestle prisoners into jail cells. He had none of the requirements needed to be an officer of the law, but he profoundly admired Walter Thurston. For Sheriff Thurston, that was enough. When townsfolk questioned Thurston on his hiring Top, they were put in their place.

While Deputy Top listened as his cronies exchanged tales of a big buck that got away, Sheriff Thurston burst through the front door.

"There's a problem," the sheriff said loudly. "Forget breakfast, Deputy. Pay Betty and come with me." At the cash register, Thurston dropped the names of Wesley Birch and Jed Dawson. There was also something about an insane asylum and a death threat. It was enough fodder for the cronies to chew on but too few facts to connect the dots.

Once Deputy Top had climbed on the buckboard, he asked, "What's the rush?"

Thurston was ready to talk. He spoke of Hiram Folger letting the undertaker take Wesley from the asylum, and of Wesley running away and spewing threats against Jed Dawson, as if the newest groom in town was a dart board.

"Are we heading to the Dawson home?" the deputy asked.

Sheriff Thurston didn't reply. The deputy could tell the sheriff was thinking. They rode in the wagon from Main Street to Alpine Road in silence. Except for the usual crunching of pine nuts, only squeaking wheels were heard.

The sheriff finally pulled up on the reins. "The answer we seek is in the hobo camp."

"How do you know?" the deputy asked, regretting his question before it even left his mouth. He knew better than to question Sheriff Thurston.

"A hunch!" the sheriff replied. "The case of Wesley Birch is all but solved."

After driving two blocks south of town to the railroad tracks, the sheriff turned his horse and wagon down a side road that reached the hobo camp. The camp was in a pleasant place—a grove of cottonwood trees with a small stream covered with watercress. Leaving the wagon, the lawmen walked to the makeshift camp, which consisted of a few raggedy tents and a fire pit. The deputy looked in one tent and found it empty. The sheriff looked in another and found a pudgy hobo sleeping off his nightly escapade.

"Time to get up!" Sheriff Thurston shouted. "I've got questions for you."

The hobo got up and staggered out of the tent. "By your badge, it looks like you're the sheriff in these parts. Come to check out the hobo camp?" The hobo pointed to a log near the fire pit. "Gentlemen, sit down on my couch." The hobo plopped down on a grassy knoll near the log. "What can I do for you, Sheriff, and your trusty deputy?"

"You're new here. Haven't seen you around town before,"

Thurston said, spitting out the shell of a pine nut onto the grass. "You're the first overweight hobo I've seen."

"Genetics, I guess. I was a big baby and never got over it. Just arrived two days ago from Denver on the luxury flatcar. Won't be here long. Headed to the California beaches. I hear it stays warm all winter in Southern California. Ever been to California, Sheriff?"

Sheriff Thurston didn't answer. He was not in camp to chitchat. He gazed at the hobo as if studying every feature of his face. "We came to camp looking for help. A crazy man was in Rooster Creek last night, threatening one of our leading citizens. We're wondering if you saw any strangers around here."

"Everyone is a stranger to me," the hobo said. "What does your man look like?"

"He's short and skinny and has a long beard. Whatever he says is laced with scriptures."

The hobo stood up and kicked the coals in the fire pit before saying, "You know, Sheriff," and then he paused.

It was a pregnant pause that caused Thurston and his deputy to lean forward as if the next words were just what they wanted to hear.

"I did see a feller like that," the hobo said as he put his hand in his pocket. "I've never met such a guy. If I hadn't known better, I'd swear he was the devil himself. Not even the Pope would want him to come unto Jesus. He told me, 'There's a man in this town ten times worse than Judas.' I could tell the guy was crazy and belonged in an asylum."

"Did he say anything about a man named Jed?"

"As a matter of fact, that was the name. He compared Jed to Judas, and Judas came up short. If what he said is true, I never want to meet Jed."

"When did you see this man?" the sheriff asked as he glanced at his deputy with a look of *I told you so.*

"He came in camp last night," the hobo said. "I was in the tent just about to nod off. I came out to welcome him and see if he was hungry. He said, 'I hunger and thirst for the word of God.' In case that wasn't enough to sustain life, I roasted a potato over the fire and gave it to him. He gulped it down like he was starving."

"The man mentioned Jed. Are you sure of that?" the sheriff asked.

"He told me Jed is the one person who puts Judas to shame. He'd been up to his barn earlier in the evening. Said he planned to return to the barn today and something about Moses and an eye for an eye. He had big plans for Jed's demise, but then something really strange happened. His whole expression changed. It was like he was receiving a revelation or something. He went into a sort of trance before announcing with some authority, 'I've heard the word of the Lord. Did you hear it?' I didn't hear a thing. Before I could counter, he said, 'The Lord told me vengeance is mine.' That was it. To tell you the truth, revelation and all that mumbo jumbo scares me. For a little guy, he was unnerving."

"Where is he now?" the sheriff asked.

"He's on a train."

"How do you know that?" the sheriff asked.

"He asked me what time the next train came through town. I told him right away but the train only slows down in Rooster Creek; it doesn't stop. He asked if the train slowed down enough for him to jump on a boxcar. I've had more than one friend get hurt trying that shenanigan. I told him it's dangerous and that he should wait until the morning ten o'clock train heading to Vegas. That train comes to a complete stop."

"I don't have all day to listen to you," the sheriff said.

"He told me he'd take his chances. He said, 'If I fall on the tracks, I fall into the arms of Jesus. Glory, hallelujah.'" About two o'clock this morning, I ran with him to the station with his beard being whipped by the wind. The train slowed. I stopped to catch my breath—being slightly overweight has zapped my energy. The bearded man didn't stop. He sprinted to the train. I've seen elk and deer run fast, but nothing was as fast as that skinny man last night. He caught hold of the boxcar. Last thing I saw, he was standing in a boxcar shaking one shoe and shouting to the heavens, 'I dust off my feet and curse Rooster Creek.'"

"Sounds like our man," the sheriff said, standing up and stepping forward to shake hands with the pudgy hobo.

"If I'd known you wanted him, Sheriff, I would have kept him in camp. That man will cause trouble somewhere, but not in your town. He's riding the rails to California. Sure hope I don't meet up with him on the beach."

"Come by my house later. It's the house with a white picket fence on Alpine Road. Lucy will see that you get a sandwich." Then Sheriff Thurston turned to his deputy and said, "Case solved."

As the two lawmen walked to the wagon, Sheriff Thurston looked back at the hobo. "Hobos are quite the guys. A lot of problems have pushed them to the trains, but lying isn't one of them. I wish everyone in Rooster Creek had the moral compass of that man." Now in the mood to be chatty, Thurston continued, "When I was about your age, I attended the police academy in Denver. At the academy, I was taught the best thing a law officer can do is follow a hunch. That's exactly what I did today. I had a hunch about the hobo camp. Excuse me for bragging, but the facts speak for themselves. The case of Wesley Birch is solved."

"How do you know the hobo was telling the truth?" Deputy Top asked.

"Did you notice the hobo had a thin upper lip? If you're looking for a sign of honesty, that's it. That guy is as honest as the day is long."

Trying to learn all he could, Deputy Top asked, "Why did you go out of your way to shake hands with him?"

"Well, my boy, you can tell a lot about a man by the way he shakes hands. A firm grip is a true judge of character. That hobo had a vice-like grip."

Deputy Top sat back on the buckboard, feeling pleased, knowing that there never was nor ever had been a lawman better than Sheriff Thurston.

"I'm going to see the undertaker next and from there find Jed Dawson," Sheriff Thurston said. "I'll drop you off at the office to handle the other issues of the day. If anything important comes up, find me."

Deputy Top changed from being pleased to being disappointed in an instant. He wanted to see the faces of the undertaker and Jed when they learned Wesley Birch had left Rooster Creek.

The sheriff dropped Deputy Top off at the office and drove his wagon straight to the mortuary. He had hoped Seth wouldn't answer the door. He wanted to break it down and rescue the undertaker from his guilt. He hoped to find him curled up like a slug inside a coffin, waiting for someone to close the lid. Surprisingly, when Seth answered the door, he looked well rested. He had spent the hours with Buttercup.

"You'll want to be seated for my news and have your money jar ready," Sheriff Thurston said. "The case of Wesley Birch was solved in less than an hour."

"Where did you find him?" Seth asked.

"Not so fast. Money first, then details," the sheriff said as he popped a pine nut between his teeth and settled onto the nearest couch. "If you bring me a slice of chocolate cake and a generous helping of pudding, we can call it even."

"I'll do you one better," Seth said with a joking twinkle in his eye. "I'll bring you a bladder, two kidneys, and an intestine smothered in raspberry jam." With that, the mortician rushed to the kitchen and cut a large slice of chocolate cake and heaped on the pudding. When he returned to the parlor, Thurston had nestled himself in the couch for a long stay.

With all the pomp and ceremony of a commencement address, Thurston began his tale at Betty's Diner and ended it at the hobo camp. In between was a dramatized story of jumping on a boxcar and shaking hands with a plump hobo. Seth sat on the edge of his chair, not wanting to miss any part of the retelling.

"Thank the Lord," Seth said. "Wesley has jumped a train, cursed our town, and gone to California. Your news is more than good—it is wonderful. I feel such a relief. It is as if a huge bag of oats were lifted off my shoulders. I can't wait to call Hiram Folger and tell him the news. He'll be amazed."

The sheriff's mood changed at the mention of Dr. Folger. "I'll tell Folger," he said. "Let's go to Jed's house and tell him. At this point, he knows nothing of Wesley leaving the asylum. You might want to prepare your speech."

Sheriff Thurston and the undertaker climbed onto the buckboard and headed to the home of newlywed Jed Dawson. They were merry along the way, reminiscing about their favorite stories of Rooster Creek and concurring that none were as riveting as the story of Wesley Birch and his sister, Lydia. Sheriff Thurston complimented himself to the highest heaven for solving the case, and Seth promised him the best funeral Rooster Creek had ever seen—dancing girls from Vegas jumping out of a cake and money flowing freely on roulette wheels.

The gaiety of the moment was squelched when they neared the Dawson home. Standing on the front porch was Jed with a rifle in hand. Sheriff Thurston bolted out of the wagon like a gazelle with Seth trailing.

"What are you doing with that rifle?" the sheriff asked.

Without saying a word, Jed pointed the rifle to two chairs on the porch and motioned for the lawman and the undertaker to sit down. He remained standing with his rifle cocked.

"Have you seen the barn door?" Jed asked Sheriff Thurston.

"Which barn door?" the sheriff asked.

"Follow me. Be quick about it," Jed said.

Without any questions, the sheriff and Seth followed Jed. Etched on the barn door was the biblical phrase "An eye for an eye."

"Wesley Birch is back in Rooster Creek," Jed said. "What are you doing about it, Sheriff? If that crazy loon comes here again, he's a dead man."

"Wesley Birch has been in Rooster Creek," Sheriff Thurston said. "But he is not in town anymore."

Jed's stern expression did not change. "What are you talking about? Did you arrest him and send him back to Nebraska?"

"No! But you won't be seeing Wesley coming around here. He left town last night on a freight train heading to California."

"How do you know that?"

"A hobo told me the whereabouts of Wesley Birch at the camp by the railroad tracks. He spoke of a strange man coming into camp last night. The man talked of religion and of his hatred for you. The hobo said the strange guy jumped on a boxcar heading to California. You're safe. He's gone."

"Can you trust the word of a hobo?"

"You can trust this one. He had all the marks of an honest man."

Jed stood on one foot and then the other. He looked up and then down. He was confused and wanted direction.

"I can assure you that you're safer in Rooster Creek than a gold piece locked in a vault at Chipman's Bank," the sheriff said.

"I still can't figure it out," Jed said. "That man wanted to take my life. He wanted revenge for his sister's death. I can't see him changing his mind that quick. And how did he get back in Rooster Creek? He was locked up in the asylum."

"Seth has something to tell you," the sheriff said, passing the buck. "Shall we go up to the porch so we can all sit down?"

"Tell me here," Jed said, raising his voice and the rifle.

Unprepared to tell the story of coercing Dr. Hiram Folger to let him take Wesley out of the asylum to a man holding a loaded rifle, Seth shook his head and refused to speak.

"Speak up, undertaker, or go back to the mortuary," Jed said.

Seth cleared his throat, and, as if on cue, his shoulders slumped. "It's all my fault." He told of taking Wesley Birch out of the asylum, hiding him in the wagon bed, and of searching all night in a desperate attempt to find him. In an emotional finale, Seth told of having nowhere else to turn but to Sheriff Thurston.

At this point, Jed let out a tirade of emotions that only a man threatened with his very life could understand. He verbally whiplashed the undertaker until the sheriff pushed Jed back as if Thurston were a referee in a heated ball game.

"That's enough!" Thurston shouted. "Seth made a mistake. That's all. He's sorry."

"His life wasn't being threatened," Jed yelled. "He put my life in jeopardy and stands before me sorry. Is that it? I'm expected to forgive him for being an imbecile? No! I refuse! Get away from me, undertaker, before I use this rifle on you."

Seth had no comeback, no words to counter Jed's wrath. He walked away from the barn a broken man. He had only one thought: a wish that he had made that extra coffin to curl up in and wait for a merciful friend to close the lid.

By the time Sheriff Thurston and Jed had returned to the porch, Jed knew every detail of the story–from the hobo camp to shaking a shoe against the town of Rooster Creek. Jed had lots of questions, and Thurston had answers.

Jed still wasn't sure, however. "I need Karl to help me think this through."

"You don't need Karl Ward to figure anything out," Thurston said. "I already did. The case of Wesley Birch is closed. Karl has bigger fish to fry in Vegas. By now, he's probably as corrupt as any gambler on the Strip."

Just then, Matilda walked out on the porch. "What's going on?"

"Sheriff says Wesley left town," Jed said.

"Sheriff, are you sure?" Matilda asked. "I've been worried sick. Hardly been able to function today when I learned that the barn door had been etched with 'An eye for an eye.'"

"It's over, Matilda," the sheriff said. "No need to worry. I solved the case."

Partially satisfied with the sheriff's answer, Jed took his rifle and bullets inside. Matilda followed. The sheriff bid them goodbye and headed to his wagon. With the reins in his hands, he began to laugh. *When I get back to the office, the first thing I'll do is telephone Hiram Folger and ask to speak to Wesley Birch. After he tells me that Wesley is not in the asylum, I'll wait a few days to give him the good news.*

21

THE TELEPHONE CALLS

"Operator, connect me to the insane asylum in Provo," Sheriff Thurston said into the phone.

"Connecting you with the asylum, Sheriff," the operator said.

"Dr. Hiram Folger's office, may I help you?" Hester answered.

"Hester, this is Sheriff Thurston at Rooster Creek. I need to speak with Hiram right away. Get him on the line."

"He's in a training meeting now. Can I take a message?" Hester asked.

"This is Sheriff Thurston. I need to speak with Folger now."

"Just a moment, I'll get him."

Sheriff Thurston was smiling from ear to ear as he chewed on a pine nut and imagined Hester barging into a meeting and whispering in the psychiatrist's ear.

"Sheriff," Dr. Folger said, sounding out of breath a few minutes later. "That rooster awakened your town already? Always good to hear from you. What's on your mind?"

"Working on my report on Wesley Birch. I need to speak to him right away."

Hiram looked at the clock on the desk—not yet seven. He

stiffened. "He's probably eating breakfast about now in the cafeteria. I'll have him call you by noon." Covering the phone, Folger turned to Hester and asked, "Have you seen Seth Warenski?"

"No," Hester whispered.

"Can't wait," the sheriff said. "Have one of your security guards pull him out of the cafeteria. I'll hold the line."

Hiram reached for the stuffed chair behind the desk. Sweat was pouring in small droplets through channels etched on his face by too many birthdays.

"I sure appreciate you taking Wesley off my hands the other night," Thurston said. "I hear you put him in a straitjacket. That man is dangerous. Why are you letting him eat breakfast with the other inmates? The way he ranted on about Jed Dawson killing his sister and that 'eye for an eye' rubbish—he's crazy. It's good Wesley isn't anywhere near Rooster Creek. Put him back in that straitjacket as soon as he downs the lumpy substance you call mush. He should be picking up the phone by now. Is there a problem?"

"Well, Sheriff," Hiram said, taking a long breath, hoping to calm his nerves. "I don't think there is a problem, but Wesley's not here."

"Couldn't hear you clearly, Hiram. Did you say that Wesley is not in the asylum?"

"He'll be back any minute."

"Any minute? You know better than that. The Salt Lake boys will shred that so-called medical license of yours quicker than I can crack a pine nut. You'll be hopping on freight trains and begging food from the doors of little old ladies before the sun goes down."

The silence on Hiram's end of the phone was deafening.

"Hiram, Hiram, you still there? Get me Wesley Birch now."

The droplets on Dr. Folger's face had turned into puddling streams. Hiram stammered and tried to speak. He stammered out something about Seth Warenski and Charles Dickens and it being a far better thing that he had done, but most of his words were incoherent.

Sheriff Thurston did not reach out to provide comfort. He

relished the moment, imagining the know-it-all doctor begging for mercy. After letting that thought sink in like a sweet morsel, Thurston shouted into the phone. "Wesley Birch has been in Rooster Creek and has written 'An eye for an eye' on Jed's barn door. The boys in Salt Lake are looking for a reason to oust you. This is it."

With that, the sheriff hung up the phone, feeling smug and proud of himself for putting Dr. Folger in his place. He envisioned Hiram Folger reaching with a trembling hand for medicine in his top drawer and telling Hester that he suddenly didn't feel well and would be spending the day at home curled up like a bug facing the wall. The sheriff cracked a handful of pine nuts between his teeth. "This is a beautiful day."

JED DAWSON HAD no such feeling about the day. He needed his friend Karl. They hadn't parted on the best of terms, but now was not the time to quibble about differences. Jed reached for the phone.

"Operator, this is Jed Dawson. Connect me to the Boyd Law School in Las Vegas."

"This will take a moment. Please wait," the operator said.

"You're calling Karl?" Matilda asked. "Why? The sheriff said Wesley is gone. You're safe."

Jed ignored her.

"William Boyd Law School, Sarah speaking. How can I help you?"

"I need to speak with one of your students—Karl Ward. It is an emergency."

"Just a moment, please." After a full minute had passed, Sarah returned to the telephone. "Karl Ward is in our early morning criminal justice class now. Can I give him a message?"

"Have him come to the phone. Tell him it's Jed."

As more minutes clicked off, Matilda tried to comfort Jed and assure him that Wesley was long gone. Jed was not in the mood for her reasoning and asked her to go outside.

"I want to talk to Karl alone," he said.

Suddenly Karl's voice came over the line. "This had better be good," Karl said when he finally reached the phone. "I have a big test tomorrow, and the professor is giving a review. I have wanted to talk to you anyway. You told me that I should push thoughts of Wesley to the background and find a dancing girl. Well, she's not exactly a dancing girl—carries placards announcing dancing girls—but she's gorgeous, beyond gorgeous, unbelievably beautiful. Why, the men at the dance hall hooted and hollered more for her than any dancer on stage. I haven't gone on a date with her, but sort of. We're going out tonight. If this is what love is—bring it on."

"Wesley is out of the asylum," Jed said.

All talk of Ann Golding stopped as if it were never spoken. A chill ran through Karl's veins. Hearing the name of Wesley Birch filled him with a fear like none other.

"Listen, Karl," Jed said. "The mortician took him out of the asylum. He ran away. He carved 'An eye for an eye' on my barn door. Sheriff Thurston said a hobo told him Wesley jumped a freight train for California last night."

Karl turned as ashen as a sheet and sat down on the nearest chair.

"Can I get you a drink of water?" Sarah asked.

Karl didn't glance in her direction. All he could say was, "Go slow."

Jed tried to recall every detail but was nervous and scattered in his speaking. He shifted his weight from one foot to the other, stammered, and more than once interjected with, "Oh, yeah, there was also..."

"So the sheriff believed a hobo?" Karl asked. "Hobos have a network that runs the length of the rail lines. If a hobo thought another was in trouble, he would lie to protect him, even if Jesus Christ were standing in front of him. I wouldn't swallow the word of a hobo."

"The sheriff didn't at first," Jed said. "But when he questioned the hobo, the man knew everything about Wesley. He knew Wesley quoted scripture nonstop and stuff like that."

"Maybe Wesley had a change of heart and doesn't want to harm you, but then again... It does sound like he's really gone," Karl said. "Go back to the part about Wesley jumping the train around two in the morning."

"Like I said, the train slowed down, and Wesley jumped on and shook his shoe and cursed me and the whole town of Rooster Creek."

"Wait a minute," Karl said. "It doesn't make sense. Remember when we were in high school and would stay out all night down at the train tracks to smoke and hang out? We would watch the trains coming and going and count the cars. No matter which night we were at the tracks, the trains ran on the same schedule. The night trains never slowed down or braked as they went through Rooster Creek. They just kept on rolling. Wesley couldn't jump on a train that didn't brake."

"The hobo told the sheriff that when the train slowed, Wesley jumped on," Jed repeated.

"There's no way that could have happened," Karl said. "Wesley never jumped a train. He's still there. He's still in Rooster Creek."

"That can't be."

"Check the train schedule. Talk to Sam at the station. Maybe I'm wrong. I hope so. Check with Sheriff Thurston, too. If I'm right about the trains, you're in danger." Karl said. He then paused before saying, "We should have told the truth."

"I'll phone you back. Wish you were here." With that, Jed hung up the phone.

Karl clung to the phone as if Jed were still speaking.

"Anything I can do for you?" Sarah asked Karl. "Emergencies are always difficult."

There wasn't room for Sarah's compassion or time to return to the classroom to listen to the professor drone on about the intricacies of criminal justice. Karl's mind raced from one scenario to another, trying to reach a conclusion that would calm his fears. Finding none, he left Sarah's office muttering, "I have no other option." Important books and papers on his desk would wait for a janitor to put them in the lost and found. Karl ran to the parking lot, intent on going to Rooster Creek.

But first, he wanted to get a message to Ann Golding. He started his car and drove straight to the women's boardinghouse near the train station. At the boardinghouse, he jumped out of the car, ran up the steps, and pounded on the door. A sleepy landlady answered and demanded to know the reason for the early call.

"The girls won't be down for breakfast for at least another half hour," she said. "Come back later."

As the door was closing, Karl frantically said, "I need to speak with Ann Golding. It's urgent."

"She'll be downstairs in half an hour. Come back then."

"I can't wait," Karl said.

"You'll have to. We have house rules. Might as well make yourself comfortable."

Reluctantly, Karl sat down on the porch, but he was far from comfortable. His mind whirled through a maze of ideas, looking for an option besides driving to Rooster Creek. He could board the ten o'clock morning train, but that would mean waiting three hours. If he drove and stopped for flat tires, an overheated radiator, and gasoline, he could still beat that train, but what a hassle. Then he remembered the freight train that left Vegas for Utah at eight o'clock. It usually had a couple passenger cars attached. He'd have to hurry to catch it, but what about Ann? He'd miss picking her up. What if another drunk approached her? She shouldn't walk the streets of Vegas alone at night.

He took a note card from his vest pocket and wrote, *Ann, can't see you tonight. Going to Rooster Creek. Crazy man threatening friend. Here's money for a taxi. Karl.*

Karl knocked again on the boardinghouse door, this time even louder. Once again, the sleepy landlady appeared.

"I told you to wait half an hour. No more knocking, or I'll call the cops."

"Give this note to Ann Golding," Karl said, handing the landlady the note as if it were as precious as gold. Taking several dollars out of his wallet, he added, "Give her this too."

The landlady brightened at seeing the money. As greed filled the seams on her face, Karl told her that he was a law student and would pursue legal action if any dollar did not make it into Ann Golding's pocket. He counted every dollar to emphasize his point and wrote the dollar amount on the card.

The landlady grabbed the money and slammed the door.

Back in his car, Karl drove straight to the train depot. Whether or not he could get a ticket on the freight train was unknown. Whether he could save Jed from Wesley was also unknown, but he needed to try.

"MATILDA," Jed yelled, forgetting that he had asked her to leave the room. "Where are you?" He found his wife seated on the front porch, dabbing her eyes.

Marriage hadn't been good for Matilda. Dreams had been scattered in less than a week. Jed was allusive at best and at worst unkind.

Failing to notice her unhappiness, Jed said, "I'll be back in half an hour. Stay inside."

"It doesn't make any sense," Matilda said. "Sheriff Thurston..."

Jed left the porch in a dead run to the barn, leaving Matilda in mid-sentence. There was no time for him to look at the photograph. He jumped on Eliminator, saying, "Come on, boy. This is a race like no other."

Five minutes had not passed before Jed pushed open the door to Sheriff Thurston's office.

"Karl says night trains don't brake in Rooster Creek," he shouted.

Irritated at the intrusion, Thurston said, "I won't have that know-it-all interfering in a closed case. I told you already. Let me say it slower so there will be no mistaking my words—Wesley Birch is in California."

"You can't be satisfied with the word of a single hobo. Look out the window," Jed said, pointing to the window in the outer office. "See that hobo carrying a knapsack? He's probably headed to my house to beg a sandwich off Matilda. Does he look trustworthy to you?"

"Come on, Jed. Settle down. Wesley jumped the train."

"Go with me to the station. Let's talk to Sam and check the train schedule. Let's find out if night trains make stops in Rooster Creek."

"There is no need to check schedules," Thurston said. "The train stops every night in town like clockwork. Karl needs to save his legal training for the courtroom and leave solving crimes to me. This is my business, not his." The sheriff took a deep breath, sighed, and in slow, deliberate words, continued, "How many times do I have to tell you? The case is solved—no need to bring it up again. Wesley Birch is sitting under a palm tree at a beach in Southern California. The trouble with Karl is that he looks beyond the mark when the answer is as plain as your nose. Now go home."

Anyone watching Jed would have thought he was the one attending the Boyd Law School as he walked a pace closer to the sheriff's desk. "What does the hobo look like?"

"Let's get this straight," Thurston said, leaning back in his chair. "I'm not on trial here. But if appearance is so important to you, the hobo has dark curly hair and is heavy around the midsection and upper body."

"That's the hobo I saw walking down Main Street with a knapsack."

Opening the door, he said, "Let's go pick him up. We can take him with us to the train station."

"Jed, calm down. I don't need to interrogate that hobo again. Wesley Birch's case is closed."

Jed moved toward the door. "Either come with me or don't. But I'm going to the train station."

"Jed, you're as irritating as Karl," the sheriff said, reaching for his Stetson hat and grabbing a handful of pine nuts to put in his pocket.

Jed flew out the door and shouted back at the sheriff, "I need to know for sure."

"Hold up," the sheriff said. "I'm coming. We'll ride together in the wagon."

The sheriff and Jed rode side by side on the buckboard without a word between them. When they reached the station, both men hurried inside to speak with Sam.

"Hey. It's my friend with the slowest horse in town," the stationmaster said to Jed. "How's old Eliminator doing—ready for the glue factory?"

"We didn't come to talk about horses," the sheriff said. "We've got a question for you, Sam. When night trains pass through Rooster Creek, do they brake? Do they slow down so a hobo could jump on a flatcar?"

"Night trains? Night trains don't brake—they don't slow down. They nearly fly past this place," Sam said. "You'd have to be fast as lightning to jump on one of them. Never seen anyone try."

Jed was the first out the station door. The sheriff walked behind him, slower than usual. His swagger was gone. There was a clear danger in Rooster Creek, and he had missed it.

"Hurry up," Jed yelled. "You've got a job to do, Sheriff. My life is in danger. Matilda's life could be in danger too."

22

THE STANDOFF

"You left the office unattended," Sheriff Thurston said to Deputy Top, as the deputy entered the office. "I've warned you about that."

Deputy Top ignored the implication of incompetence. "Mrs. Crosby's cat got stuck in the maple tree again. I think that cat sharpened her claws since last time I got her down from that tree," he said, checking the scratched holes in his shirt. "Anyway, how did Seth and Jed take the news about Wesley hopping a train to California? You solved the biggest case to hit Rooster Creek since Mr. Crosby clubbed old man Johnson for stealing his water. The Wesley Birch case is the talk of the town."

"Hold my calls," the sheriff said. "I'll be in my office."

The sheriff slammed his office door shut. The ride from the train station, with Jed harpooning him at every turn for believing a hobo, had been infuriating. *It won't be long before the men at Betty's Diner will be chewing on that morsel.* Thurston sat down behind the desk and tried to come up with a plan. Although Jed Dawson had moved to the top of his most disliked men in town list, Thurston had a legal obligation to protect him. The question was not how to protect the man who infuriated him but how to protect him without staining his own reputation as the best lawman in Utah. No matter how Thurston turned the scenario over in his mind, the spin had to be that he didn't believe the hobo. He could say that he pretended to believe the hobo to keep Matilda and the other women of Rooster Creek from being unduly concerned. That was a good spin but not good enough.

While Sheriff Thurston mentally considered one scheme after another to turn the Wesley Birch case in his favor, the phone rang.

Deputy Top answered. "The sheriff can't be disturbed. He's put in a full day already solving the Wesley Birch case." There was a pause before the deputy spoke again. "You're a reporter from the *Deseret News* and want to interview the sheriff about Wesley Birch?"

Covering the phone, Deputy Top called to the sheriff. "You'll want to take this call, Sheriff. It's a reporter from the *Deseret News*." Returning to the phone, the deputy said, "He'll be right with you."

"Sheriff Thurston here," Thurston said after he picked up the phone in his office.

"Sheriff, I just got word that you solved the case of a runaway from the asylum today. That's worthy of the front page."

"Well, there's one loose end to tie up," Thurston said. "Let's talk tomorrow, and I'll give you an exclusive story."

"Thanks, Sheriff. I'll call back first thing in the morning."

Thurston opened his office door. "No more calls, Deputy, and that's final!"

It was not until he had downed a whole bag of pine nuts that the sheriff figured out the right spin to the Wesley Birch case. He'd never believed the story of the hobo. He knew evening trains didn't stop or even brake at Rooster Creek. He played along with the hobo, knowing that the hobo would lead him to Wesley Birch. For their safety and to make it appear authentic, he told the undertaker and Jed Dawson that Wesley jumped on a flatcar out of town. Through his undercover work, Wesley was captured, and, once again, the best lawman in Utah saved the day.

Feeling smug about reaching the perfect spin, Sheriff Thurston now turned his attention to protecting Jed until he caught Wesley. He walked into the outer office and told Deputy Top to go to Betty's Diner and deputize his cronies at the counter.

"Send each man down a different street to find Wesley, and be quick about it," he ordered. "Most of them will remember what the madman looked like from the wedding reception—small skinny man with a long beard. He's easy to spot. Call me when you find him. I'll stay by the phone in case a reporter from the *Tribune* calls."

"Hold on, Sheriff. Wesley jumped the train," the deputy said.

"It's complicated," the sheriff said. "Are you going to the diner, or do I have to go myself?"

Deputy Top hurried out the front door and walked at a fast clip to the diner. He had more questions than answers but didn't want to raise the wrath of Thurston.

Jed's side of things was dramatically different than that of Sheriff Thurston and Deputy Top. Jed had never felt more exasperated with any person than he did with Sheriff Thurston. Not even the Lehi basketball player who'd purposely tripped him during a game came close to Rooster Creek's sheriff. Jed was red-hot mad, knowing Thurston's failings put his life in jeopardy. There was no cordiality when the sheriff pulled the wagon up to his office, and Jed got out.

Without so much as a goodbye, Jed untied Eliminator and jumped on the horse's back. In a huff, he kicked in his heels, and Eliminator took off. Without incident or even a wave to townsfolk, Jed raced down Main Street to his cottage. When he arrived home, he jumped down, tied Eliminator to the fence, and ran up the walk. Yanking the door open, he called, "Matilda, Matilda, where are you?"

"I'm here," Matilda said, somewhat guarded, still unsure where she stood in their relationship. "Did you find the answer you wanted?"

"Wesley didn't leave Rooster Creek!"

"How do you know that?" Matilda asked. "Sheriff Thurston told us…"

"I went with Thurston to the train station. Sam says evening trains don't brake or slow down as they pass through town. Wesley didn't jump on an evening train."

"Oh no!" Matilda said. "The madman will hunt you down because he thinks you killed his sister."

As fear took over, Jed glanced around the kitchen as if looking for a solution to his problem. With a jolt, he saw that his rifle and bullets were missing. "Where's my rifle?" he asked Matilda. "Did you put it someplace?"

"I haven't touched your rifle," Matilda said. "It's right where you left it this morning."

"It's not there," Jed said. "Did anyone come in the house?"

"No, but a hobo knocked on the door and wanted a handout."

"What did he look like?"

"Curly dark hair and stocky."

"That's the hobo I saw walking past the sheriff's office this morning. I asked Thurston to pick him up for questioning. That excuse of a sheriff wouldn't do it. Did the hobo come inside?"

"No. I fixed him an egg sandwich and handed it to him on the porch, but there was something odd. Without leaving the porch like the other hobos do, he sat down and ate the sandwich. As I watched, I saw him lean over to see inside the kitchen. He asked me if you're a hunter like Nimrod. I thought that was a strange question. I felt slightly unnerved. Then the phone rang. I went to the parlor to answer it. It was your mother on the line. She was calling to say that she'd heard that Wesley Birch had hopped a train to California and wanted to express her relief. She also wanted me to know how lucky folks were in Rooster Creek to have a lawman like Sheriff Thurston. When I came back to the kitchen, the hobo was gone."

"He must have come into the house and picked up the rifle and bullets while you were talking to my mother. Did you see which way he went?"

"No. Like I said, he was gone before I got back to the kitchen."

"I wish Karl were here. He'd know what to do," Jed said. "Wish I was a praying man. Afraid those Sunday school lessons didn't take. I sure need the Lord on my side."

"We should get out of Rooster Creek for a few days," Matilda suggested.

"We're sitting ducks in this house," Jed agreed. "The sheriff should have sent a platoon of deputies to protect me, but we obviously can't count on the sheriff. Could we stay with your sister in Lehi?"

"Kathryn would welcome us with open arms," Matilda said. "I'll phone her right now."

"Tell her we're on our way," Jed said. "Throw a few clothes in a carpetbag. I don't know how much we'll need. We may be at her house for a while. I'll take Eliminator to the barn, feed him, and hook him up to the wagon. I'll be back within half an hour. Don't open the door to anyone. And stay away from the windows."

Matilda felt very nervous and wished Jed had paused long enough to embrace her.

Instead, he kept instructing her. "If I'm not back in half an hour, call the sheriff 'cause I'm in trouble." With that, Jed ran out of the cottage to the fence and untied Eliminator. With his trusty steed at his side, he walked at a fast clip to the old Ward barn. He filled a bucket with oats, and, for one fleeting moment, he thought of his beloved Lydia. Jed didn't know when he would return to Rooster Creek and see her beautiful face in the photograph and remember the night they'd kissed at the Rigby Hotel. Jed carefully pushed aside some hay and lifted a floorboard. Underneath the board was a Montgomery Ward catalog with the photograph tucked inside. Jed gently pulled the photograph out of the catalog and stared at it, hoping that past remembrances would never fade.

"She was gorgeous," he said aloud.

"Is that a photograph in your hand?" The voice came from the dark corner of the barn.

Startled, Jed whirled around. In the shadows, nearly hidden from sight, Jed could see the outline of a hobo with curly hair holding a rifle.

"What are you doing in here?" Jed asked. "Get out."

"Let me introduce myself to you, Jed Dawson, the liar of Rooster Creek, the man who makes Judas blush." The hobo removed the black wig and stepped into the light. "My name is Wesley Birch. You killed my sister, Lydia, the woman you pledged to marry. You have married another in her stead but will never be happy, for you long for Lydia. Drop the photograph and move slowly with hands held high toward the wall. Don't turn around."

Jed's heart pounded as he slowly dropped the photograph and lifted his arms. "Wesley, I didn't kill your sister," he said. "I wasn't going to marry her. You've got it all wrong. The bridge was wet from the morning dew, the horse slipped, and the three of us plunged into the raging river. I saved your life. I have sorrowed deeply over not saving Lydia. The sorrow has enveloped me. I sorrow as much as you. Be reasonable."

Wesley's face flared with anger as he swung the barrel of the rifle upward and pulled the trigger. The bullet was not intended for Jed; it was a call for townsfolk to gather. It took only one bullet at midday to summon the men. Although no man outside the barn knew for certain why the shot was fired, all knew it meant trouble for one of their own.

The only person who knew the reason for the rifle shot was Matilda. The half hour had come and gone without Jed returning to the cottage. She screamed with fear the second the shot reverberated in her ears and then reached for the telephone. "Operator, this is an emergency. Connect me with Sheriff Thurston."

After three agonizing, long rings, the operator said, "Go ahead, please."

"Sheriff, this is your niece, Matilda. Jed went to the barn. He hasn't come back. I heard a rifle shot."

"I heard it too," Sheriff Thurston said. "Stay away from the windows. I'm coming."

The sheriff grabbed his gun and bag of bullets, then ran outside. At the same time, Deputy Top was just returning to the office after deputizing the men at Betty's Diner.

"Spread the word," the sheriff yelled at him. "Have the men meet me at Mr. Ward's old barn on Jackson Street."

With that, the sheriff jumped on his horse and rode to the Ward barn.

It did not take long for a crowd of men to gather near the barn. They were the same men who had listened to Seth Warenski's Sunday school lessons and Bishop Bailey's calls to repentance. They were the same men who elected Mr. Ward as town mayor and gawked as the undertaker threw Wesley Birch to the ground outside the dance hall. They were not all friends and had disputes that stemmed back to their grandfathers, but, on this day, each had a rifle and was ready for battle. Like a convoy of soldiers on the move, they circled the barn, waiting for an order to attack.

From where Wesley was standing, he could look through a peephole. He gave Jed a blow-by-blow account of men in the crowd.

"Sheriff Thurston's here. He's wearing a blue Stetson hat, hardly appropriate for the occasion. He's motioning with his arms and telling everyone to move back. No one is listening. The mortician is here. I like Seth Warenski; he tries to do the right thing. He made a stately cross for Lydia. Oh, here comes Matilda. I haven't seen her since the reception. She is a jilted wife for nothing more than a photograph. She looks distraught. Still cares for you—foolish woman. There's old man Johnson. I hoped he'd come. Bishop Bailey has stepped forward and is trying to help the sheriff move the crowd back. Not having any luck."

Without warning, Wesley fired the second shot. The men, who

boasted of saving Jed, ran for cover. Some thought Thurston ran faster than any man in Rooster Creek.

When Wesley was sure that silence reigned over the barnyard, he shouted through a crack in the barn. "'Suffer the little children to come unto me.' You've come. Welcome, sinners. Wesley Birch is my name. With me is Jed Dawson, the night clerk at the Rigby Hotel. He won't be going to the hotel tonight. He and I have other plans."

"Wesley, you are surrounded," Sheriff Thurston shouted. "Put down the rifle and come out of the barn with your hands up."

"I can't see you, Sheriff. Hiding? Oh, there you are crouching down by the granary. And you thought I couldn't see you. Afraid of a hobo? Surely not a fat hobo with curly black hair." Then Wesley turned back to Jed. "We'll need to wait awhile. Can't go forward until Hiram Folger joins us, and it wouldn't be right to leave out your friend Karl. I thought he would be the first here."

As an hour passed, Wesley intermittently shot the rifle and laughed as he watched men run for cover. Occasionally, he blurted out scriptural verses about patience and Armageddon. He kept the men in the barnyard on edge by preaching about the teachings of Moses, 'An eye for an eye,' and singing hymns. All agreed that Wesley had the competitive edge over Bishop Bailey when it came to scripture bashing. They also agreed that they had never heard *Amazing Grace* sung better.

After an hour of guns cocked and occasional scriptural threats, Sheriff Thurston shouted, "Wesley, for the last time, you are surrounded. Put down the rifle and come out of the barn with your hands up."

Nothing happened, even though the sheriff repeated his message the next hour and the next.

"What shall we do?" men in the crowd asked him, saying, "You're in charge."

A few suggested ramming the barn door, climbing on the roof, and standing in place and shooting. The only idea Sheriff Thurston could not shake was waiting until Wesley fell asleep so Jed could overpower him.

By lunchtime, women brought baskets of food and blankets, though none of the women stayed long except Matilda. She was planted, always staring at the barn, looking for some sign of Jed. There was a chill in the air, but no man was going home. There was a madman in the barn with a rifle, and Jed Dawson was in trouble.

23

THE BARN

Hiram knew better than to pull back the covers and climb into bed, but he couldn't help himself. *Sheriff Thurston was right. The boys in Salt Lake will make a big deal about me letting Wesley Birch leave the asylum. My years of service to the psychologically impaired will abruptly end with no applause.* The psychiatrist wished he had never let the mortician take Wesley Birch to Rooster Creek. He wished that he had never read Charles Dickens. But more than that, Hiram wished he was a better man.

A few hours of such thinking plummeted the psychiatrist into a deep abyss not unlike how his patients suffered. But unlike them, he knew how to pull himself up to face life, come what may. It wasn't the slow route of counseling to peel back layers of disappointment and regret to reveal the core of the problem. Hiram knew there was a better way. It was simple, really: confront fears and come out the victor.

Trying to move from his bed of unhappy musings, Hiram played mind games until he shoved his fear of the boys in Salt Lake to the back burner. With renewed confidence, he threw off the covers and sprang out of bed, telling himself there was no challenge so great that he could not accept the consequences. He lost round one with Sheriff Thurston in his attempt to cover up a mistake, but he wouldn't lose round two.

Freed from the mental constraint to court the favor of the good old boys in Salt Lake, Hiram's thoughts turned to Wesley—his patient lost in a realm between fantasized revenge and the real world.

"I'm going to Rooster Creek for a few hours," Hiram called to his wife. "Need to fix a problem."

Without dropping a stitch in her embroidery, his wife replied, "You're good at fixing problems. I'll have dinner ready when you get home."

Hiram tied his horse to the buggy and headed to Rooster Creek. He enjoyed the first part of the journey—the splash of colors in the autumn leaves and the frolicking clouds overhead. As he drove through small towns, he was more cheerful than in the past few days. When a friendly person passed by, he deflected questions about the asylum and only spoke of fall leaves and the bountiful harvest, for this was his day, the day Hiram knew where he stood and embraced it.

It was not until he was passing Pleasant Grove that he heard talk of a madman holding a young man at gunpoint in Rooster Creek. Details were sparse, but Hiram had no doubt the madman was Wesley Birch, and the young man was Jed Dawson. He picked up a few more tidbits from farmers who called to him from their fields. When Hiram entered Betty's Diner on Main Street in Rooster Creek, he finally learned specific details about the situation. A strange chill ran from his head to his toes as he listened to Betty recount the day at the barn. Hiram felt feverish and dizzy all at once.

"Can I have a cup of water?" he asked Betty.

When he felt slightly better, Betty gave him directions to the barn. The barn was easy to find in a town that was awakened by one rooster. However, Hiram was surprised to see the number of men carrying rifles and circling the barn like wolves stalking prey. He looked for Sheriff Thurston in the crowd. Luckily, the sheriff was easy to spot. He was waving his arms and shouting for the umpteenth time, "Move back!" Hiram could see no one was listening to him.

Hiram got out of his buggy and stepped lively to the back of the granary where Sheriff Thurston stood.

"Dr. Folger has come," Wesley said to Jed. "We almost have a full complement. Only your accomplice is missing. What's keeping Karl? I'm ready to pull the trigger."

Jed had grown restless standing against the wall. Fear he'd felt at first was replaced by agitation. He sized up Wesley and knew he could overpower the skinny man given the right opportunity.

"Sit on the floor and cross your legs," Wesley said to Jed. "You'll be more comfortable. I insist."

The new position was not advantageous to Jed.

Wesley Birch was not the only man to notice Hiram Folger enter the barnyard. When Sheriff Thurston saw him approach the granary, he yelled, "It's about time you got here. Look at the mess you caused: Jed held captive by a madman on vacation from the asylum—a vacation approved by you, I might add."

"I deserve that," Hiram said.

"I told you to keep him locked inside your spooky fence. You defied an order from an officer of the law. I could lock you up, but why? The boys in Salt Lake will crucify you."

Hiram smiled tightly, moved away from the sheriff, and slowly walked toward the barn.

"Come back, Hiram, you fool," Sheriff Thurston shouted. "What are you doing? Retreat!"

Wesley watched the psychiatrist slowly approach the barn door. "Oh my!" Wesley said to Jed. "What have we here? It's Hiram Folger from the asylum. Dr. Folger has been like a father to me the past few days. If you had the chance to know him better, you'd have liked him too. He knows how to talk to crazies and liars. Which are you, Jed? You killed the very woman you pledged to marry. You knew the bridge was wet." Wesley paused before saying, "Dr. Folger will ask me how I feel about what's happening with an emphasis on the word *feel*. He'll listen carefully as he tells me I'm like a son to him, and that he misses me at the asylum. He'll try to persuade me to return with him to insanity behind the great fence. The good doctor forgets that being wronged trumps anything else."

As Hiram approached the barn door, he asked, "Can you hear me, Wesley?"

"I can hear you, Dr. Folger. Is this a social visit or a clinical exam?" Wesley asked, pointing the rifle in the doctor's direction.

"Wesley, my son," Hiram said, "I've come to take you home. This is no place for you. Rooster Creek isn't your home. Provo is your home. I've reserved the auditorium for your performance Wednesday night of *Dr. Jekyll and Mr. Hyde*. Posters announcing the play have been placed in every dormitory. The cooks have agreed to provide popcorn."

Turning to Jed, Wesley said, "Dr. Folger is really good. Did you notice how he built on a positive to get me to relinquish a negative? What he fails to grasp is 'An eye for an eye' performance starring a madman with a rifle is a better show than *Dr. Jekyll and Mr. Hyde*."

Not hearing a response from Wesley, Hiram continued, "Holding a grudge creates a self-inflicted wound. You know that, Wesley. Let it go."

At this point, Hiram touched the barn door with his left hand and motioned with his right for Sheriff Thurston to join him. The sheriff took a few steps toward the barn as Wesley tightened his grip on the rifle and pulled the trigger. Hiram Folger fell to the ground.

"I didn't come this far to walk away," Wesley shouted. "Send someone to carry Dr. Folger's body. You'll find no bullet holes in the doctor. It was fear that sent him tumbling to the ground. Take him from the barn; his body is stiffening."

Two men in the crowd rushed to the barn, lifted the psychiatrist to his feet, and dragged him to safety behind the granary.

"Wesley," Sheriff Thurston yelled. "You can't go around scaring men to death. Tell me in plain English what you want."

"My wants are simple. I ask for little."

"You don't have the upper hand here," Sheriff Thurston said, pulling his gun from the holster. "We are tired and want to go home. You're out of bullets. Come out of the barn with your hands up."

"Always a step ahead, aren't you, sheriff?" Wesley laughed. "Just a slight miscalculation. I have a bag of bullets!" Wesley pointed the rifle in the air and shot again.

The sheriff fell backward, complaining of chest pains.

As the day progressed, others got up the courage to walk to the barn. Seth Warenski sobbed as he walked. All he could talk about was not wanting to prepare Jed's body for burial. Next came Bishop Bailey, who had prepared a sermon while standing in the barnyard. He pulled out a piece of paper and read to Wesley of the Lord's mercy. When he started quoting scriptures and said *thee* instead of *thou*, Wesley was tempted to blow off his head. The most dramatic walk was taken by Matilda. She might have gone the distance if Sheriff Thurston had not insisted that she go home.

"You go home," Matilda yelled. "Take all the men with their rifles too. Not one of them is doing any good. What is your plan to get Jed out of the barn?" When the sheriff did not reply, Matilda said, "I'm going in the barn to get Jed out."

Matilda then moved across the open barnyard with a look that meant business. Seth tried to restrain her. He had thrown Wesley to the ground outside the dance hall, but he could not stop Matilda. Those who saw the attempt made wagers and lost. Matilda was a strong woman and would not be stopped by a wiry undertaker. She shouted profanities at Seth that shocked even the men who spent the wee hours of the morning in the saloon.

"Calm down, Matilda," Sheriff Thurston said. "You're a woman. Act ladylike." Then, angered by the crowd of men inching forward to see Matilda in action, the sheriff shouted, "Move back! You have no business being here. Go home and take Matilda with you."

The men stepped back a few feet, but none were about to go home or tangle with Matilda.

"Sheriff," Mr. Crosby shouted, "could you deputize the men to come over to my place and help me dig a cesspool?"

"Crosby," the Sheriff said, "you can be so irritating."

Inside the barn, Wesley listened to it all. "Here comes your jilted bride," Wesley said to Jed.

"Matilda?" Jed asked and started to stand.

"Not so fast," Wesley said. "Your place is on the barn floor with the other rats. Matilda is walking fast. She's a woman with a purpose."

For the first time that day, Wesley felt a hint of fear.

Matilda pounded on the barn door. "Wesley, you harm my husband, and I'll tear you apart. Open this door, or I'll rip the barn down. Don't think I won't. When I get my hands on you, you'll wish you never stepped foot in Rooster Creek. Jed, take him. What are you waiting for? Deck him! We've waited long enough."

"Matilda, go home," Jed called out. "This is my problem, not yours."

"You tell her, Jed," Wesley said. "We don't want Matilda near the barn."

It took the sheriff and three or four other men to remove Matilda from the barn door. She was as mad as a hornet and flung her arms wildly, hitting Deputy Top, who yelled, "She broke my nose."

Attention given the deputy and his nose was short-lived as the sound of horse hooves pounding the dirt rose with intensity. The crowd, almost in unison, turned to follow the sound.

"It must be Karl," Wesley said to Jed. "He's riding to your rescue like Sir Lancelot. He plans to save the day. So pompous."

"Karl's coming to the barn?" Jed asked.

Karl had never taken much to horses and was holding on for dear life while prodding Sam's horse to go faster. When the stallion turned into the barnyard, Karl, now riding side saddle, slid off. He landed on his feet but only for a moment.

Getting a good look at the inept rider sprawled out on the ground, Sheriff Thurston threw his Stetson hat to the ground and muttered under his breath. "As if we didn't have enough problems today, that know-it-all Karl Ward has come back from Vegas. Too bad the stallion didn't drop him like a bug."

Mayor Ward, Karl's father, rushed to his son's side. "How did you hear?" he asked.

Breathless, Karl told of Jed's phone call, bribing the stationmaster in Vegas to let him catch the eight o'clock freight train, getting off the train in Rooster Creek just minutes before, and learning from Sam that Jed was being held in the barn by a madman.

"Sam let me borrow his horse," Karl said. "What have I missed?"

Mr. Ward talked of gunfire and of Dr. Folger, Seth Warenski, Bishop Bailey, and Matilda approaching the barn. Even though others were eavesdropping on the conversation, he spoke of Sheriff Thurston's inability to control a crowd and his failure to devise a plan to save Jed. "The only plan I've heard the sheriff has come up with is to wait until Wesley falls asleep. He thinks Jed will rise up and take the rifle from the madman."

Karl shook his head. "The sheriff has the brains of a slug."

Pretending not to notice Sheriff Thurston coming his way, Karl walked directly to the barn. He was red in the face and boiling with anger.

"He's mad, all right," Wesley said to Jed. "I'm not afraid of him. I have truth on my side. Karl thinks he can outwit me. Oh, the follies of unchallenged youth."

"Wesley, I know you," Karl shouted as he approached the barn. "You are a coward. You hide inside the barn, feeling smug, knowing that a hundred men with rifles can't make a move or else Jed dies. But you are nothing but a small, skinny man with no hope and no future. I'm coming in. Shoot away."

"I hold a photograph in my hand," Wesley shouted. "Know anything about a photograph? It's a wedding photograph of Jed and my sister, Lydia."

"Name your terms, Wesley," Karl said, moving closer to the barn door.

"Tell the truth."

"I lied to you, Sheriff Thurston, and to Seth Warenski. Is that what you wanted to hear?"

"An eye for an eye," Wesley answered. "The moment has come. No more delays. As a prelude to 'An eye for an eye,' I'll sing for the last time, 'Amazing Grace.'"

As he sang, the circling men quieted and inched forward with their rifles aimed at the barn. None joined in the chorus, but Wesley knew they wouldn't, for this was the crescendo, and he had the starring role.

As the last refrain ended, Wesley shouted again. "Is Jed, the night clerk of the Rigby Hotel, willing to admit he lied? Will he admit that he was going to marry my sister? Will he admit that his reckless speed caused her death?"

There was a great pause, and in that pause, Wesley knew that he had every eye and every ear turned to the barn.

"Karl, you're free to leave the barn door," he said. "You will suffer more by living than if I shoot you right here."

Karl tried to push the barn door open, sweating with the effort.

"Don't try that again," Wesley shouted. "You're testing my patience."

"Jed is innocent!" Karl yelled. "Let him go."

Wesley fired the rifle. All eyes were riveted on Karl. He didn't flinch.

"Mercy cannot rob justice," Wesley shouted. "Jed Dawson, confess or die!"

"I've told the truth, Wesley," Jed said. "I had no plans to marry your sister. I told you that I was marrying Matilda. You would not listen. You were ranting outside the hotel about me marrying your sister. It was an impossible situation. I admit to pushing Eliminator too fast. It is my fault the buggy slipped on the wet bridge. I saved you from drowning and tried to save your sister. That's the truth."

"I have only three bullets left. The sun will soon go down. Before it does, justice will receive her due. This is the last time you'll hear my voice. God bless us all."

Not even the chill of the wind could fill the silence that fell like a smothering blanket over Rooster Creek. All hope was gone. Evil had triumphed.

Bishop Bailey walked over to Sheriff Thurston and asked, "Would it be all right with you if we had a prayer?"

"Prayer is the only thing that could save Jed now," Thurston said.

"Normally," Bishop Bailey said, "I would call on Mayor Ward, but we don't have that long. If it is all right with you, Sheriff, I'll pray."

The sheriff nodded.

"Dear God, this is not a time for words. We need help. We need a miracle. Amen."

24

A MIRACLE

ydia awoke before daylight with thoughts of Karl. He was no
Jed Dawson, but who was? Karl had a laugh and a quick wit
few could match. And, if the truth be told, Lydia had never met such
a man. His strong stance against the drunk coming on to her and his
joke of the wedding chapel were memories that begged for attention
until the sun's rays heated her room. Lydia stretched and pulled back
the blanket. She stepped out of bed, hurriedly dressed, and rushed
downstairs to breakfast. The landlady was waiting for her.

"Fancy pants left this for you," the landlady said in a loud,
crackling voice as she handed Lydia a piece of paper. As if an
afterthought, she added, "He also left you money." The mention of
money caused the young women seated at the dining room table to
look up. With a sweaty hand, the landlady reached into her fraying
apron pocket and pulled out a fistful of crisp dollar bills—fifty-three
dollars, to be exact. The women gasped as if on cue. Fifty-three
dollars was more than their monthly wage.

"Why did fancy pants give you so much money?" the landlady
asked. "What did you do to earn it?" With a knowing smile, she said

with a firm tone, "We don't allow that kind of behavior in the boardinghouse."

When the young women giggled at the dark innuendo, Lydia's face flushed with embarrassment. She reached for the note and the money and ran out of the dining room, up the stairs to her bedroom, and slammed the door. She hastily opened the note and read, *Ann, can't see you tonight. Going to Rooster Creek. Crazy man threatening friend...* She swallowed a lump in her throat as the embarrassment turned to ominous fear. She crumpled the note in her hands and threw it against the wall. She knew what the message meant—her brother, Wesley, was threatening Jed. The weighted memory of leaving her brother asleep in the mortuary while she ran to the train station felt even more heavy now.

Lydia's mind raced from past fears of Frank Cromwell to the landlady's innuendo, trying to assure herself that her choice to come to Vegas was best for all concerned. But no matter which way she twisted the scenario, her decision to leave Wesley behind to threaten Jed was the wrong choice. Feeling desperately alone with no one to turn to, Lydia stood, opened the door, and walked down the hall to the bathroom. The image in the mirror startled her. She picked up a towel and tried to wipe away the darkness that had formed around her eyes but could not. She took a deep breath and returned to her room.

Kneeling by her bed, Lydia prayed, "You don't know me, but you know my brother, Wesley. He quotes your good book all the time. For his sake, please keep Jed safe. Please, dear God, help me do what is right."

Lydia rose from her knees, no different from when she had knelt. Believing that fresh air might clear her thinking, she left the boardinghouse and walked to a nearby park. While seated on a park bench littered with last night's riotous living, she had conflicting thoughts:

I could catch the ten o'clock train to Utah.

I could get off at Rooster Creek.

I could find my brother.

When Wesley knows it's me, he will fall at my feet, believing he is seeing a resurrected being. But he will no longer threaten Jed.

By showing up in Rooster Creek, the kind mortician will lose his undertaker's license. No one will trust him again.

Karl will know about Jed, and Jed will know about Karl.

Matilda will be distressed.

I'll be labeled a liar.

Gossips will have a field day.

Confused but becoming ever more resolute, Lydia left the park bench and started walking toward the train station, slowly at first. As she moved ever closer to it, she quickened her pace. Once inside the train depot, she purchased a one-way ticket to Rooster Creek with a portion of Karl's money. When the conductor shouted, "All aboard," Lydia was the first to step off the station platform onto the train.

The train ride to Rooster Creek was fitful, much like her earlier ride to Vegas. As the train passed through one quaint town after another, Lydia thought of being free from her crazy brother. Now, all she could think of was returning to Wesley's grasp. It was only a week since she had left him sleeping in the mortuary. As she reviewed her week, Lydia was surprised that Karl again entered her mind. She recalled meeting him at the diner and his insisting on taking her to the boardinghouse and leaving money for her to catch a taxi.

When her mind returned to Wesley threatening Jed, she feared arriving too late in Rooster Creek to prevent Wesley from attacking the man she would love forever. When the train hissed and screeched into the station at Rooster Creek, Lydia hurried along to the Rigby Hotel, hardly noticing that the weather had turned cold.

When Lydia entered the hotel lobby, Mrs. Rigby was seated behind the desk.

"Welcome. Did you just arrive on the train from Vegas?" Mrs. Rigby asked.

"Yes," Lydia said. "I am wondering if you know the whereabouts of Jed Dawson?"

"Normally, I wouldn't be here at dusk," Mrs. Rigby said. "Jed is the night clerk. He would have been here if a madman were not holding him hostage at gunpoint in a barn."

"Can you give me directions to the barn?" Lydia asked.

"You're not thinking of going to the barn, are you? The crazy man has been firing a rifle all afternoon. It has me unnerved—frazzled. Each time that gun goes off, I think the madman has killed Jed. All the menfolk in town are standing outside the barn waiting for orders to attack. They have rifles too. It's like a war zone over there."

As if Mrs. Rigby hadn't heard her, Lydia said in a slightly different way, "I would like directions to the barn."

"Oh, please, dear, you really shouldn't go. It's no place for a woman. I hear the menfolk are getting pretty heated up. You want a room?"

"Perhaps, but first, directions to the barn," Lydia said.

Mrs. Rigby paused before saying, "You're making a big mistake, dear, but if you must, the barn is two blocks to the east, past Betty's Diner. Follow the wagon and horse tracks. I strongly advise you to stay away. There was gunfire about half an hour ago."

Although tired and scared, Lydia took a deep breath and went outside. She walked past the diner and continued east a couple of blocks before she saw a crowd of men. She was not diverted by their guns or boisterous talk. With sheer determination, she walked toward them. She knew they saw her when the men went silent. Lydia did not look to the right or the left. With head held high and shoulders back, she made her way to the clearing between the crowd and the barn.

As she walked in the clearing, the sun was at her back, and a light swirled around her, making it appear that her light pink dress was white, and her auburn hair was as fire.

A feeling of reverence overcame the men as they watched her walk. Some fell to their knees, sure they were seeing an angel. She was so graceful that others claimed she wasn't walking—she was gliding.

From his peephole in the barn, Wesley saw the angelic woman approach. There was a familiarity about the way she moved and held her head high, but nothing more.

When Lydia was within thirty yards of the barn, Wesley fired the rifle. The men ran, but not Lydia. She kept walking. The possibility of death was not a deterrent. The light reflecting from the barn was all that stood between Lydia and the barn door.

"Don't come any closer," Wesley called out.

Lydia kept moving. Upon reaching the barn door, she whispered so only Wesley could hear. "I'm on the Lord's errand, Wesley."

There was no reply.

"What is she saying?" Sheriff Thurston asked before yelling to the woman, "Speak up! We all want to hear."

Lydia faced the men and held her hands in the air before putting her finger to her lips as a sign of quiet. Turning to the barn, she whispered, "Are you there, Wesley?"

She waited for an answer. There was none.

"Wesley, it's your sister, Lydia."

"Lydia?" Wesley whispered.

"It's time to catch the train heading to California."

"You drowned at the bridge. I fixed your hair."

Lydia finished his sentence. "Just like mother would have done."

"I have the wedding photograph of..."

"Me and the night clerk."

Jed could hear the whispering. He laughed to himself. *Only Karl could contrive a rouse so clever.* Jed slowly moved from a sitting position to a crouching position, ready to attack.

"Lydia, have you risen from the dead? Did you see Father and Mother?" Wesley asked. "Tell me something about myself that no one else would know."

"You can quote scriptures better than Father."

Visibly shaken by the response, Wesley took his finger off the trigger.

Jed sprang to his feet and rushed the madman. He knocked the gun out of his hand, grabbed the photograph, and threw Wesley to the ground.

"Let him be," Lydia whispered.

"Fat chance," Jed replied. "He's a dead man."

"Is he dead like me?"

Quickly, Jed looked out the knothole. Then taking a step back said, "Lydia, it's you."

"Bring Wesley out of the barn and give him to me."

The barn door opened as dusk faded into darkness. The men could barely see Jed carrying a man slung over his shoulder, yet a deafening cheer arose from every corner of the barnyard.

When the roar died down, the woman faced the men and said, "Wesley is mine. Remain where you stand."

Jed set Wesley on the ground and pushed him toward Lydia, who looked up at him and whispered so no one else could hear, "It's over, but I will love you forever. I'm leaving with Wesley. Keep the men away from us."

With that, Lydia took Wesley's hand and calmly walked into the darkness.

Sheriff Thurston began to follow them, but Jed put a stop to that. "It's over," he said to the sheriff. "Back off. I've had a hard day."

Jed ripped up the photograph before facing the crowd and saying, "Gather close to me, especially Matilda." Matilda rushed to his side. They embraced.

"I have a story to tell," Jed said. "It's a story of romance, mystery, and an angel. The story begins with a brother and sister checking into the Rigby Hotel and a night clerk who spent the evening with an angel."

As the story progressed, Seth was relieved that Jed did not know that he had buried an empty casket. The part of Sheriff Thurston popping pine nuts was fun, but the sheriff didn't like Jed making fun of his Stetson hats. The men laughed. The superintendent of the asylum allowing an inmate to have a vacation to visit a grave was absurd, as was the part of the bridegroom being held captive in a barn by a hobo.

None walked away from the story, for each had played a role. It was not until the train whistle was heard in the distance that Jed wrapped up. "Go home! I want to be with Matilda."

The men left the barnyard in a jovial mood, knowing they had a story that trumped any told by their wives.

Before Karl left, Jed said, "I look forward to hearing about the dancing girl of yours."

"She looked a lot like the angel who walked to the barn," Karl said. "For a moment, I thought she was Ann Golding."

The two friends laughed.

As for Lydia and Wesley Birch, they boarded the train leaving Rooster Creek. Lydia got off in Vegas and looked forward to Karl's return. Wesley went on to California. There is some question as to his whereabouts after reaching Los Angeles. Some say he settled in Huntington Beach and spent his days calling sunbathers to repentance. Others say he opened a restaurant in Hollywood with a man in an orange-checkered suit who took photographs of customers. The most reasonable scenario has Wesley completing an education at Claremont and being hired as a religion professor at Brigham Young University, a mere twenty-five miles from Rooster Creek. As the scenario goes, Wesley spent his days on campus and his nights in the Provo Asylum, where he occasionally put on plays for the patients. A crowd favorite was always "An Eye for an Eye."

ACKNOWLEDGMENTS

Surrounding ourselves with friends whose irrational behavior, strange ideas, odd mannerisms, and side-splitting humor has provided just the right material for us to develop the character of Wesley and his adversaries. To our many unusual friends, none more than Katie Ritchie patiently edited our rewrites when sane editors were looking for an exit.

ABOUT THE AUTHORS

George Durrant is a creative writer who just happens to be handsome and in love with Susan. George was reared in American Fork, Utah. He enjoys watercolor painting, writing children's stories, and sports. Although he is more comfortable with a paintbrush in hand, he has written nearly forty inspiration/self-help books. He married Susan because he believed she deserved the very best.

Susan Easton Black is known far and wide for her scholastic research and writing. Over 100 books attest to her ability to address one fact after another. It was a stretch for Susan to reach beyond the facts to discover Wesley. She credits George with opening a door to the wonders beyond reality.

This has been an
Immortal Production